DEATH LIST

Following a prison murder, a hitman targets the police

JOHN DEAN

Paperback published by The Book Folks

London, 2019

ISBN 978-1-7939-8444-9

www.thebookfolks.com

Death List is the sixth novel in a series of British murder mysteries featuring Detective Chief Inspector John Blizzard. Details about the other books can be found at the end of this one.

Chapter one

It was in the early hours of the morning that George Killick's wretched existence was brought to an end. The prisoner was shaken roughly from a troubled sleep by a hand gripping his shoulder. For a few moments, he did not know where he was and struggled to make out features in the inky darkness of the cell. Something was pressing down on his face and Killick started to fight for air, fists clenching, legs thrashing frantically, mouth unable to call for help, his only sound a muffled scream.

'Shut the fuck up, you nonce,' hissed a voice.

It was the last sound that George Killick heard before death overcame him. Once he had stopped struggling, his cellmate waited for a few moments until he was sure that his victim was dead, then removed the pillow from his face and sat in silence on the edge of the bed, listening hard in the darkness, straining for any sound that might indicate that anyone in the adjoining cells had raised the alarm. Nothing, just the fitful noises of a prison at night. And who would dare to raise the alarm anyway?

When he was certain that the job was done, Mark Roberts climbed on to the top bunk and lay in silence. A career burglar, he had done some terrible things in his life, things that had traumatised his victims, but he had never taken a life and he was surprised how little it had affected him now that he had finally done it. His lack of concern was probably, he reminded himself, because George Killick deserved to die after what he was threatening to do. Everyone had agreed that he needed to be silenced and no voice had been raised in opposition when the task was given to Roberts. The code was the code and no one broke it.

'Bastard deserved it,' murmured Roberts just before sleep finally overcame him. 'No one likes a grass.'

It was a short slumber as, within a couple of hours, he heard the sound of Hafton Prison coming to life with the officers opening the cells for slopping out. Listening to keys turning in locks, the clang of heavy doors, the holler of prison officers' voices and the protestation of inmates, Roberts composed his thoughts and prepared to play his part. He had rehearsed it enough times in the days leading up the murder and, as the cell door was unlocked and swung open to allow light to flood into the room, he started shouting until one of the warders entered the room to find him standing by the bed, staring down at the prone figure of George Killick.

'Shit,' said the officer.

* * *

An hour later, Roberts was standing in the assistant governor's chilly office on the ground floor of the Victorian building, flanked by two grim-faced prison officers.

'And you heard nothing?' asked the assistant governor, a weary-looking, balding man sitting behind a large oak desk. 'A man dies and you hear nothing at all?'

Roberts shook his head.

'I'm a heavy sleeper,' he said.

'Even so, I would have thought you might have heard a man dying in the bunk below you.'

'Well, I didn't, Mr Halford. What was it that did it for him then, a heart attack?'

'That's what the doctor suspects,' said the assistant governor gloomily. 'Killick had a history of heart problems. Nothing that would suggest something like this, though.'

'Stress.' Roberts nodded wisely. 'He was terrified most of the time. Everyone knows what they do to nonces in a place like this. Stress like that can do terrible things to a heart, I reckon.'

'Yes, well when I need your expert medical advice, I'll ask for it,' said the assistant governor and gave him a hard look. 'Are you sure you did not hear anything?'

'I told you, first I knew was when I woke up and found him dead. I'd have raised the alarm if I had heard owt, but I didn't.'

'OK,' sighed the assistant, flapping a hand in the direction of the door. 'On your way.'

Roberts left the room and headed up the stairs, trying not to make his smile too obvious as the warders let him through a series of doors and out onto the second-floor landing. As he made his way towards his cell, a number of inmates approached him and, having ensured that the warders were not watching, patted him on the shoulder or shook his hand.

'Bastard deserved it,' said one.

'What you going to do with the money?' asked another.

'Dunno,' said Roberts. 'Haven't really thought about it.'

But he had thought about it. A lot. A fast car, that's what he would buy when he got out. The money would be enough to get himself a decent set of second-hand wheels and he'd drive out of Hafton and wouldn't look back.

Chapter two

Before you ask, I wasn't sad when I heard that George Killick was dead nor did I feel any sense of responsibility about what happened to him. Sure, I'd heard that he was having a tough time in prison, men like him always do, but how could I feel any sympathy? Putting his kind away is the job and he knew what he was doing when he abused those children. George Killick knew what the consequences would be when we finally caught up with him – and he must have known that we would catch up with him eventually. I know they thought they were beyond the law but George Killick must have known that one day there'd be a knock on the door and one of our officers standing there waiting to arrest him.

Anyway, this isn't about the death of George Killick, is it? Not entirely anyway. No, this is about my death. Time to get it all out in the open and bring an end to the secrets. Even though it all happened just a matter of days ago, it already seems a long way off. The past, they say, is another country and sitting here recounting my tale to you it feels like it. But you are right – my story must be told. And it must be told to you, whether I like it or not. You, of all people, have reason to hate me for what I have done and, after my tale is told, you must decide how best to punish me.

It was just past three in the afternoon and the winter sun was sitting low and bright in the cloudless sky when the car left the suburbs and headed into the rural flatlands on the western fringes of the city of Hafton. After ten minutes on an uneven A-road, the driver guided the vehicle onto a narrow hedge-lined lane. Within a few minutes, he had turned off again, this time onto a rough track leading through a copse.

Acutely aware that the car was visible from the lane, the driver steered carefully down the muddy track before coming to a halt in the middle of the trees and switching off the engine. After sitting in silence for a few moments, he reached for the pocket book lying on the passenger seat and flicked it open at a page. He did not need to read what was written – he had read it so many times – but somehow seeing the list of names stiffened his resolve for what he was about to do. Three of them. He rested his forefinger on the first name. Alex Mather. Did he deserve what was about to happen to him? Did any of them deserve to be murdered in cold blood? Even the coppers? The man knew that rights and wrongs counted for nothing; he had no alternative but to carry out what he had agreed to do. He felt the tears start in his eyes and he wiped them away with the back of his hand before alighting from the vehicle and slipping the book into the back pocket of his jeans.

Glancing round to check that he was still alone, he listened intently for the best part of a minute but heard only a lone crow cawing in the canopy above. Then another sound, the distant drone of a vehicle engine. Mather. Still a mile away, he reckoned. Plenty of time. He reached back into the car and opened the glove compartment to reveal a handgun. Having checked that the weapon was loaded, he locked the vehicle and started walking briskly back towards the lane, slipping the weapon into his coat pocket as he went and conscious all the time of the noise of the engine growing louder.

* * *

If Alex Mather knew that he was being watched as he approached the copse, the detective constable did nothing to let it show; he did not flick the car's brakes, did not glance across at the man leaning on the gate, did not even look in his rear-view mirror as he left him behind. But Alex Mather *did* know that he was being watched; it was just that his years as an undercover police officer had taught him not to react. Reacting, he had learned, was the way to get yourself hurt, but a decade living a double life had given the detective a sixth sense when it came to danger and the man at the gate was trying far too hard to appear casual. Nothing stood out more to Mather than someone trying to look natural; the detective had always believed that it was his ability to look like he belonged that had kept him alive.

The detective constable did not recognise the man except to see that, like Mather, he had slim, short brown hair, was fresh-faced and clean-shaven. Unlike the detective in his smart grey suit, the man was dressed in jeans and a scuffed parka. When the detective judged that the man was far enough away not to notice, he allowed himself a glance in the rear-view mirror. The man was watching the car.

Mather wondered what to do and frowned. Uncertainty was a new sensation for the detective. More used to trusting his instincts, he knew that they had begun to fail him as the pressure had mounted during the final months undercover. Experience may have taught him to sense danger but eventually it had turned him into someone who jumped at loud noises and peered nervously into the shadows for assailants who were not there. His vigilance had morphed, without him noticing, into paranoia and it had taken John Blizzard to recognise the warning signs.

Rebuking himself for over-reacting and having driven for another minute, the constable saw a grubby white cottage set back from the lane, only visible between the trees because the branches were still bare. He smiled. It was the same reaction every time he arrived home. He liked the thought – home was not a word he had been able to use for the best part of a decade as he drifted from one squalid bedsit to another.

Mather turned off the lane and eased the car up the rutted drive that led to the cottage. Having parked the car in the rickety timber garage, he repeatedly rattled the padlock to ensure that it was secure, something he had found himself doing more and more. It was locked, he knew it would be, but obsession had been taking a grip of his mind since he came out from his undercover life.

Checks completed, he stared pensively across the bare fields towards the deserted lane. Alex Mather had much to think about. Bringing his undercover days to an end the year before might have solved one concern but it had caused another. He had found routine CID work unfulfilling and, in a way he did not quite understand, he missed the constant danger. That afternoon, he had spent an hour with his DCI discussing his plans to leave the force. It was time to move on, Mather had told Blizzard. Time to leave the city, make a clean break, find Polly and the kid. Maybe make up with them before it was too late. If they'd have him. The discussion had found no resolution and the two men had agreed to meet again in the morning but by the time he arrived home, Alex Mather's mind was made up.

He let himself into the cottage and walked into the kitchen, where he removed his jacket and hung it over one of the chairs at the table. His mobile phone rang. The detective took the call.

'Mather.'

'You're in danger,' said a man's voice.

'What do you mean? From whom?'

'I can't tell you but watch yourself, that's all. There's someone out to kill you. And not just you.'

'Who else?'

'I can't say anything else. Where are you?'

‘At home.’

‘Well, get the fuck out of there. Go to ground.’

The phone went dead and, five minutes later, having hurriedly packed an overnight bag and walked back into the kitchen, Alex Mather cursed as he remembered that he had forgotten to lock the front door when he walked into the building. As he did so, he heard the click of the latch. Sometimes, he thought bleakly, the figures in the shadows were real.

* * *

‘So, is Alex serious?’ asked Arthur Ronald, looking across his desk at John Blizzard. ‘Will he quit the force?’

‘I am afraid he might, yes,’ said the detective chief inspector, taking a sip from his mug of tea. ‘Unless we think of something to change his mind pretty damn quick.’

It was late afternoon and the light was starting to fade as the two men sat in the detective superintendent’s office at Abbey Road Police Station, a collection of prefabs that had been erected as a temporary measure but were still there three decades later.

‘And what *would* change his mind?’ asked Ronald. ‘I don’t want to lose a good officer without trying everything we can to keep him.’

‘Nor me but he’s pretty fucked up and we have to take our share of the blame for that.’

‘Yes, but …’

‘No buts, Arthur. He became too exposed and we did not support him.’

‘Less of the we. Neither of us were his handlers, remember. That was down to Andy Barratt and his team. They were the ones who dropped the ball. It was not our responsibility to look…’

‘Oh, come on, Arthur, that’s no excuse and you know it! I saw Alex enough times in those final weeks to know what was happening.’

'Yes, and you were the one who raised the alarm, remember,' said Ronald. 'Not his handlers. They did not have a clue how close he was to the edge. If you had not intervened, there's a good chance that he would be dead by now.'

'Nevertheless...'

Blizzard did not complete the sentence and silence settled on the office. It was not a hostile silence; they had been through too much together over the years for that. They did, however, react very differently to conflict. Ronald, a pudgy, balding man with ruddy cheeks and eyes with bags which sagged darkly, was the diplomat, the calm one who smoothed out the crumples, moderated his language, put out the fires. Blizzard, dishevelled, hair tousled, dark suit crumpled, tie at half-mast, was the one more likely to have started the fires. The one with the reputation.

'So where did you leave it?' asked the superintendent, reaching for his tea and sighing as he discovered that it was now lukewarm. 'Any resolution?'

'I said we should sleep on it.' Blizzard gave a dark laugh. 'Some hope.'

'Baby Michael playing up?' said Ronald with a smile; he remembered the old John Blizzard who frowned on officers who admitted to problems in their private lives.

'Yeah, he is,' said a weary Blizzard, who had just become a father for the first time. 'Fee says it's colic. Every time he gets to sleep, he's grizzling within minutes.'

'Ah, I remember it well,' said Ronald, a father of two teenaged children who was now more worried about mortgages and university costs. 'Give me a mutton-headed thug over a grouchy baby any day.'

'Amen to that.' The superintendent glanced at a piece of paper on his desk. 'OK, let's forget Alex for the moment. Where are we with the mugging? Last thing we want is some toerag waving a knife at old dears, especially with the crime stats the way they are. I want him stopped.'

'David is going to talk to one of his informants. See what he knows.'

'The chief asked about him again this morning. Still wants him to go for promotion. There's a uniform post over at Cradley, if he wants it. The chief's view is that you can't stay a detective sergeant all your life.'

'I keep telling you, Arthur, he does not fancy going back into uniform. I think it's my lovable personality that keeps him in CID.'

Ronald gave him a sceptical look.

'Yeah,' he said, 'that'll be it.'

* * *

Alex Mather stood in the kitchen and surveyed the man pointing the handgun at him with a mixture of fear and curiosity. During his last six months undercover, the detective constable had found himself increasingly preoccupied by thoughts of death, where and when he would die and who would be the one to end his life. It had become a morbid preoccupation. Now that the moment seemed to have arrived, the detective felt strangely calm. One of them had to be, he decided, and the fact that the gloved hand clutching the gun was trembling was not lost on the detective constable. This was not a pro, he concluded, not someone used to handling firearms. Looking at the shaking hand, Mather was not sure if that was a good thing or not.

The detective stared at the face and tried to remember if he had seen him before. It was certainly the young man he had seen leaning on the gate but the more he studied the features, the more Alex Mather was convinced that they had never met. He had always thought that he would be killed by someone he knew and for a reason that he could understand. Something worth dying for. The young man with the shaking hand and the beads of sweat glistening on his brow offered neither option.

'Do I know you?' asked Mather eventually, relieved that his voice sounded calm and assured.

'You know who sent me,' said the man, tightening his finger round the trigger. 'He wants to make sure you don't tell anyone what you know.'

'Know about what?'

'Enough talk,' said the man.

* * *

'I take it you heard that George Killick died last night?' said Ronald, looking across the desk.

'Not sure there'll be many mourning his passing,' said Blizzard. 'Natural causes, I heard. Heart attack.'

'The prison doctor confirmed it this afternoon,' said Ronald. 'Killick was under a lot of stress. He'd taken very badly to prison, didn't feel safe even though he was in the special protection wing.'

'Oh, dear, what a pity. Every cloud, eh…?'

'Cynic.'

As Blizzard picked up his empty mug and prepared to leave the superintendent's office, Ronald glanced at the clock on the wall. Twenty-five past four.

'Why don't you knock off early?' he said, noting his friend's heavy movements. 'You look done in. I'm sure Fee would like you back for the little un's bath-time, especially if he's been twisting all day.'

'I would do,' said Blizzard, heading for the door, 'but some damn fool of a superintendent wants the monthly crime stats on his desk by five o'clock.'

'How are they shaping up? Not down again?' Ronald looked worried. 'We can't afford another lot like last month, John. The chief won't be happy.'

'Yeah, yeah, I know. I've got David doing some number-crunching as we speak. He's better than me at…' The inspector's voice tailed off.

'Better at what?'

'Better at computers.'

'You'd better not be trying to fiddle the stats,' said Ronald, fixing him with a stern look. 'I know they need to look good but the last thing we want is the chief thinking that we are trying to mislead him.'

'Who, me?' said Blizzard with his best innocent look. 'Such a thing would never even cross my mind. I have far too much respect for our esteemed leader.'

'Yeah, sure you do. Anyway, do them tomorrow.'

'If you're OK with that,' said Blizzard.

'I'm OK with it,' said Ronald, adding as the inspector disappeared into the corridor, 'and don't worry about Alex. These things have a way of sorting themselves out. I'm sure everything will be fine.'

'I'll hold you to that,' replied Blizzard and walked towards the CID squad room.

David Colley was the only detective in the office, sitting at his desk by the window, hunched over a computer keyboard on which he was laboriously typing one-fingered. The detective sergeant was more than a decade younger than Blizzard and much sharper in appearance. Tall and lean, the detective sergeant had black hair without a sign of grey, which was neatly combed as always. His round, almost boyish face, was clean-shaven, his black trousers, blue shirt and grey jacket were all perfectly ironed and beneath the desk his black shoes gleamed.

'You need glasses,' said Blizzard, noticing how close his colleague was to the screen.

'Yeah, I know. Where have you been?'

'With the Super. He's worried that we may be cooking the books.'

'Less of the "we",' said the sergeant. 'Anyway, don't worry, they're all above board.'

'He says he doesn't need them until tomorrow.'

'Now you tell me,' grunted the sergeant. 'Mind, I'm just about finished.'

'They look any better?' asked the chief inspector, slumping wearily into a chair and putting his feet up on the desk. 'God, I hope so.'

'Overall crime up one percent again.' Colley gave him a sly look. 'Not great but possibly just low enough to keep you in a job for another few weeks.'

The inspector knew that there was truth behind the sergeant's quip. Blizzard had been Arthur Ronald's first appointment when the superintendent assumed command of CID in the force's southern area, which included Western Division. Many senior officers had challenged the wisdom of promoting the abrasive drugs squad officer but Ronald brooked no opposition and, reluctantly, the chief constable backed his judgement. It was a judgement that had seen the best crime reductions in the force, a record built on a zero tolerance approach to crime. The first rise in a long time the previous quarter meant that questions were being asked and both Arthur Ronald and John Blizzard were feeling the pressure.

'I am not sure anything will satisfy the chief,' said Blizzard with a sigh. 'It was bad enough when the local rag reported the last lot. Too many villains letting their mouths run off. I tell you, David, we've got to get a grip.

'Time for a Blizzard Special maybe?' asked Colley, running his finger down a line of figures on the screen as he did his final checks. 'Kick down a few doors? Drag a few out of their beds. That always goes down well with the media and the chief loves all the media attention.'

'Not a bad idea. Just need a good reason and I'm not sure some toerag waggling a knife at a pensioner is going to do it. Any word on that?'

'I went looking for my informant but he's not at any of his usual haunts.' Colley gave him a puzzled look. 'In fact, none of my guys have been around the last few days.'

'Same here and even when I did track down Sammy B this morning, he couldn't get rid of me fast enough. I know I'm not exactly his favourite person but he's not usually that willing to give me the brush-off.'

'Maybe something's afoot.' Colley looked up from the figures. 'A big job, maybe?'

'If it is, I have no idea what. Oh, while I remember, the chief has been bending Arthur's ear about you again. He's got an inspector's job going at Cradley. Wants you to go before the promotion board.'

'You know my views on going back into uniform, particularly somewhere like Cradley. Too many sheep. I take it you've heard that George Killick is dead?'

'Yeah, inwardly I'm weeping.'

'He'll certainly not be missed. How'd it go with Alex? He wouldn't tell me, just did his mean and moody act.'

'Not good.' Blizzard lowered his feet, walked over to the window and stared out at the car park. 'We should have done more to protect him, David. I mean, ten years undercover, that's enough to turn anyone's mind.'

'Alex knew what he was getting into.'

'But he lost perspective and someone should have seen it.'

'You saw it.'

'Maybe. Anyhow, he's determined to quit the force. Says he can't handle the routine stuff. Gets bored.'

'I know how he feels,' said Colley, scanning the figures on the screen. 'If I have to deal with another bloody shed break-in, I'll go bonkers.'

The sergeant hit a button on his keyboard with a flourish and walked over to the printer as it wheezed and started to churn out pages.

'Anyway, you can have these now,' said the sergeant. 'And I wouldn't worry about Alex. We must be due a nice juicy murder soon. Maybe that's what's in the air. Cheer us all up, I reckon.'

'Must recommend you for Crime Prevention should you ever put in for promotion,' said Blizzard.

'Don't you dare,' said Colley.

* * *

The gamekeeper was halfway across the field when he heard the shot. He frowned – it was not someone after crows with a shotgun. Too small a calibre. A second shot rang out and the gamekeeper glanced round, trying to place where it came from. All he could see was the cottage a couple of fields away but nothing appeared out of the ordinary. The gamekeeper waited for another shot but it did not come. He shrugged, clicked for his dog to follow him and started walking again.

In the cottage, the gunman stood for a few moments, shocked by the noise of the weapon in the small kitchen. Then, galvanised by the thought that someone might have heard, he walked over and stared down at the prostrate form of Mather, blood rapidly pumping out from his chest to stain his white shirt front. To the man's horror, the detective was still alive, his skin grey, his breathing shallow, a gurgling noise emanating from his lips. The man knew what he must do but something deep inside prevented him firing the fatal shot. Mather would die anyway, he thought, and a third blast would only increase the risk of attracting someone's attention.

He walked over to the window and went rigid as he saw in the fading light the gamekeeper walking across the far side of the field, a shotgun over his shoulder. Ducking low to avoid being seen, the man peered out, heart pounding hard and fast in his ears. He watched with growing relief as the figure did not break stride but walked in the opposite direction from the copse and climbed over the dry-stone wall to disappear from view. Breathing coming easier, the man took a last look back at Alex Mather, slipped the handgun into his anorak pocket and hurried from the cottage.

Chapter three

'So much for something in the air,' said Blizzard as he and Colley stood in Mather's kitchen that evening and watched the forensic officers dusting the furniture for fingerprints. 'Who found him?'

'His sister. She's gone with him to the hospital.' Colley glanced at the crimson stain on the carpet. 'Found him lying on the floor with a bullet wound to the chest.'

'How did the gunman get in?' Blizzard glanced towards the window. 'Any sign of forced entry?'

'The windows are all secure and the front door was unlocked when the sister arrived. She reckons that was unusual.' Colley pursed his lips. 'That's what's weird about it. You know how paranoid Alex is about his security and it's been getting worse since he stopped his undercover work. Yet he leaves the front door unlocked. I've only been round here a couple of times but he locked the door behind us both times when we left.'

'Maybe he knew his attacker,' said Blizzard, crouching down to examine the blood. 'Do we know when it happened?'

'Four or fiveish. He'd been lying there for several hours, according to the ambulance guys. Frankly, it's a bloody miracle the man is still alive. They reckon that if the sister hadn't arrived when she did, he'd be dead.'

'I didn't even know he had a sister.' Blizzard straightened up and grimaced as his right knee cracked. 'Did you?'

'Course not. Always been one for secrets has our Alex. Something tells me we are going to find out a lot more about him now – and not all of it welcome.'

Blizzard nodded. Even though the inspector had known Mather for more than ten years, he had always found the detective constable reluctant to share personal details. No more, thought the inspector, now it was all going to be played out on the front pages. Thought of the media prompted the inspector to glance across the room to the Press Officer. Blizzard scowled as he saw Alison Curry jot something down in her notebook.

'Any chance this is just a robbery gone bad?' asked the inspector, turning his attention back to Colley.

'Wouldn't have said so.' Colley glanced over to the suit jacket draped across the back of one of the chairs at the table. 'His wallet is still there, as are two credit cards and more than £50 in cash. That does not suggest a robbery.'

'What if the intruder panicked after the gun went off? Legged it without taking the money? It would be much more straightforward. Much simpler than someone targeting him for a reason.'

'Nothing about this feels straightforward, guv. And there's another strange thing.' The sergeant pointed to the overnight bag sitting next to one of the chairs. 'Full of clothes, thrown in, like he was in a hurry. Nothing folded up, toothbrush just thrown in. Where do we think he was going? He had agreed to see you tomorrow, so he couldn't have been planning anything.'

'Clearly, something spooked him.' Blizzard rubbed his chin. 'Maybe he got wind of what was going to happen. If the word was out that he was the subject of a hit, it would explain our skittish informants. We need to know who might want Alex dead.'

'Jesus, where do you start?' Colley walked over to the window and stared out into the darkness of the night. 'His information helped put away more top-level criminals in ten years than most of us get through in a whole career. I mean, I'm not even sure you can match him.'

'You're right, and we are going to need a list of all of them.'

Colley nodded gloomily.

'I thought you'd say that,' he said.

* * *

The gunman had kept a low profile since the shooting, not daring to go home; instead driving aimlessly round the countryside until darkness had long since fallen over the country lanes and his petrol gauge had slipped into the red. Reluctantly, he headed back into Hafton's western district and stopped at the bright lights of a filling station on the bypass. Feeling that everyone was watching him, the man brimmed the tank, his eyes darting nervously left and right as he sought out signs that someone knew what he had done. Gradually, confronted by a picture of normality, and struggling to reconcile people's everyday lives with the enormity of what he had just done, he relaxed a little and headed for the shop to pay for his fuel and purchase a sandwich and a bottle of juice.

Relief coursing through his veins, he had just driven back onto the bypass, sinking low in his seat on seeing a police patrol vehicle on the other carriageway, when his mobile phone rang. He pulled off onto a side road and took the call.

'He's still alive,' said a man's voice before he could speak.

'He can't be. I shot him in the chest.'

'You botched it.'

'He looked dead when I left the cottage.'

'You lost your bottle,' snarled the voice. 'He was alive when she found him.'

The man felt the sweat pooling in his palms and his head started to ache.

* * *

The inspector noticed Colley looking intently at him across the kitchen. Blizzard walked over to join him at the window and together stared out into the darkness.

'What you thinking?' asked Colley.

'I am wondering if there could be a link with George Killick's death,' said the inspector, glancing round to make sure that no one could hear. 'Because if there is, that changes everything.'

'Yes, but Alex was involved in a lot of other investigations, remember. We shouldn't jump to conclusions. Doesn't necessarily have to be anything to do with Keeper, does it? And George Killick died of a heart attack. Natural causes.'

'I guess but nevertheless it's one hell of a coincide....' Blizzard noticed that one of the forensics officers was taking an interest in their conversation.

Blizzard surveyed the officer for a few moments. Detective Inspector Graham Ross, divisional head of forensics at Abbey Road, had brown wavy hair beautifully groomed, not a suspicion of stubble on his face and was dressed immaculately in a pressed grey designer suit with red silk tie and expensive, shiny black shoes. As ever, the inspector was struck by how out of place he looked at a crime scene.

'Anything useful, Versace?' asked Blizzard.

'There's this,' said Ross, holding up a bullet in his tweezers. 'Missed Alex and embedded itself in the dresser. From a handgun. 9mm semi-automatic, I'd say.'

'Definitely not a panicker then,' said Colley. 'Someone panicking might loose off one shot but not two.'

'And it *is* the hitman's favourite,' said Ross, slipping the bullet into an evidence bag.

'It is indeed,' said Blizzard. 'So, what you thinking? Alex lets him in, leads him into the kitchen and gets shot?'

'There's no sign of a struggle and no blood trail in the lobby. Or anywhere else for that matter. It definitely happened in here.' Ross shook his head. 'The media will have a field day with this.'

Blizzard looked at the press officer.

'Have the reptiles cottoned on yet, Alison?' he asked.

'Not yet, sir, but DI Ross is right, they will love this, especially if they realise that he was an undercover officer.' Alison Curry hesitated; everyone knew how Blizzard detested the media. 'We will have to issue some sort of statement. Once word gets out, this place will be under siege.'

'OK but no press conference,' grunted Blizzard. 'Not yet anyway. I don't have time to talk to them so keep them off my back. I don't want this turning into a circus, Alison.'

'I'll do my best,' she said. 'But I'm not sure how long we can hold them off once they find out he's a police officer.'

'Do what you can.' The inspector gestured for Colley to follow him outside. 'A word.'

* * *

'So, what happens now?' asked the gunman into his mobile phone.

'You can't go after Mather again – they've got armed officers guarding the hospital. Besides, if we're lucky he won't regain consciousness. So, we stick to the plan. Move onto the next one on the list.'

'I don't think I can do this, Ronnie.'

'We stick to the plan,' said the caller fiercely. 'You know what will happen if you don't. And don't fuck this one up. I want him dead. He'll be at The Swan tonight, like we said.'

The phone went silent and the man sat in his car and started to shake.

* * *

Blizzard and Colley stood amid the police vehicles parked along the narrow drive leading down to the lane, talking in low voices in darkness punctuated only by the dim light from the kitchen window. Occasionally, the inspector glanced away to the east, across the fields to the dull orange glow cast by the sprawling city, picturesque in the still of the night but concealing dark forces, as he knew only too well. Blizzard's mind went back to Keeper, as it so often did. The operation had always had a sense of unfinished business about it, too many threats issued against the investigating officers, and the inspector had a churning sensation in the pit of his stomach as old feelings returned.

'This feels like a hit, David,' he said.

'Yes, but not a professional one,' said Colley. 'A pro would have put another slug in Alex to make sure. He wouldn't have left him alive, particularly if Alex did recognise him.'

'Unless he was disturbed,' said Blizzard.

'Disturbed? By whom?' Colley looked into the darkness, only just able to make out the faint pinprick of light from the nearest house across the fields. 'We've seen no passing traffic since we got here. Oh, tell a lie, one tractor. Besides, a pro doesn't panic – he'd have finished the job and killed anyone who stood in his way. No, this is an amateur.'

'Fair point but it could still be linked to Keeper, so, just like we've always said, we trust no one.'

'Didn't trust anyone then, sure as hell not going to start now,' said the sergeant.

'Good lad.'

* * *

'Superintendent Ronald?' asked the slim blonde woman walking into the A & E waiting room at Hafton General Hospital and sitting down opposite him.

'You must be Rachel,' said the detective, standing up. 'I'm really sorry for what has happened to your brother. How is Alex?'

'They're about to take him into surgery. The bullet is lodged near his lung.' She glanced at the armed officer standing in the corner of the room. 'Does he really have to be here?'

'Until we know who tried to kill him, yes,' said Ronald. 'Whoever did it may try again.'

She paused for a moment or two to fight back the tears then nodded her agreement.

'The nurse said that you wanted to talk to me?' she said eventually.

'Just to get some idea of what happened tonight.'

'I am not sure I can be of much help really.' She was about to continue when a nurse appeared.

'Miss Mather,' said the nurse 'They're about to take your brother into theatre. We thought you'd like to accompany him.'

Rachel stood up and shot the superintendent an apologetic look.

'Maybe later,' she said.

Arthur Ronald stood up and watched as she left the room.

'If there is a later,' he murmured when she had gone.

The superintendent's mind went back to the first time he'd lost an officer under his command, a young bobby mown down by two thieves fleeing from a supermarket car park where they had stolen a hot-hatch. A senseless death, the coroner had called it. Remembering the officers lining the route to the crematorium, many of them in tears, Ronald sighed.

'Hang on in there, son,' he said quietly.

* * *

Blizzard's new smartphone rang and he took it out of his coat pocket and struggled to select the correct buttons. Watched with amusement by Colley, he waggled it then tapped it a couple of times before putting it to his ear.

'Bloody thing,' he said, glancing down at the caller ID, 'What happened to phones you can ring people on? Can you hear me? Hello, hello. Arthur? Any news?'

'Yes, and none of it good,' said the superintendent, his voice initially faint then reverberating loudly causing Blizzard to wince and hold the phone away from his ear. 'Anything at your end?'

'Versace pulled another slug out of the dresser. Handgun. Nine mill.'

'A hit then. Got to be someone whom he provided information against. You thought of Keeper? What with George Killick dying.'

Keeper. The name they had invented themselves. They had had to devise their own name because there had been nothing official about the operation, launched in response to rumours stretching back years that Hafton's underbelly shielded a child sex ring run by influential men who ruthlessly protected themselves and had friends within the police force.

On taking command of CID, Ronald broached his concerns with the chief constable only to be told that the force was not prepared to release manpower to 'chase shadows'. The chief's unwillingness heightened Ronald's suspicions and drove him to take a decision that would have stunned those who regarded him as a cautious man, had they known about it; Arthur Ronald launched an investigation without official clearance. The superintendent brought in officers he knew he could trust: Blizzard, Colley, Mather and Max Randall from the east side. Even after the last court case, the exact nature of the investigation's beginnings remained a secret.

'We did talk about Keeper, yes,' said Blizzard. 'But it's only one among many possibilities.'

'Nevertheless, I suggest you bring Max Randall up to speed with what's happened,' said Ronald. 'You know where to find him this time of night.'

'Yeah, I know. The Swan. I'll pop in on you first, have a word with the sister.' He ended the call and slipped the phone back into his coat pocket.

'I hope it's not linked to Keeper,' said Colley. 'We broke every rule going and I, for one, do not want to end up on school crossing patrol if it all comes out.'

'Accept the chief's offer of promotion and it's where you'll end up anyway. Nice big hat. Smart uniform. Snotty-nosed kids.'

'Got one of those at home, thank you.'

'You should try having one with colic.'

'Who would have thought that one day I would stand at a crime scene discussing childhood ailments with John Blizzard?' said the sergeant with a smile. 'OK, what do you want me to do?'

'Begin on the list. Talk to the secret squirrels. Better coming from you, I'm not exactly Andy Barrett's favourite person.'

'Where will you be?'

'The hospital, then with Max.'

'Well, you be careful,' said Colley. 'We could be next on the list.'

Blizzard did not reply but looked out into the darkness towards the orange glow of Hafton. Suddenly, the night felt very cold.

* * *

Shortly after 9pm, the man edged his vehicle out of a side road not far from Abbey Road Police Station and eased into the stream of traffic. The driver glanced down at the handgun lying on the passenger seat and frowned.

Chapter four

I'm not sure I did believe that the attack on Alex Mather was about Keeper. Not at that stage anyway. Not that first evening. No one apart from the five of us knew what we had done, and Alex had gathered more enemies than most during his years undercover. Pimps, hustlers, people traffickers, drug dealers, Alex Mather had played his part in putting them all away. But Keeper was always there, a brooding presence for all of us and one that we could not ignore. They'd always considered themselves beyond the law and in the days following each conviction of a paedophile, word had reached us that there were powerful people seeking to avenge themselves. Obviously, you get used to threats in this line of work but nevertheless…

'I'm sad that we are meeting in such circumstances,' said Blizzard as he and Arthur Ronald ushered Rachel Mather into a softly-lit side room on the third floor of Hafton General Hospital. 'In fact, we did not know that Alex had a sister until tonight.'

Rachel settled into one of the armchairs and gave them a knowing smile. Behind it, thought Blizzard, was sadness and her eyes were red-rimmed from where she had been crying.

'I imagine there is a lot you do not know about my brother. I'm his sister and much of his life was a mystery to me.' She corrected herself quickly. 'Is a mystery.'

'He certainly does not give much away,' said Blizzard, walking over to the window and staring down at the lights of the night-time city centre. 'We don't know that much about his private life.'

'It was the same for the family. A few days before she died, my mother said that her one regret was that she did not get to know her son better. It's a sad thing for a parent to say about a child, Chief Inspector.'

'It is indeed,' said Blizzard. He thought of his new baby and wished he was at home instead of sifting through the wreckage of more lives; it was the kind of thought that he had been having more often since the birth.

'Alex was always like that, though,' continued Rachel. 'Even as a child, he would tell you nothing then get defensive if you pushed him.'

Recognising the description, both men nodded. Rachel fished a handkerchief out of her handbag and dabbed at eyes that were moist again. The inspector waited until she had composed herself.

'Tell me,' he said, coming to sit on another of the chairs, 'why did you go to see your brother tonight? Any special reason?'

'He rang me this morning. Said he had something he wanted to discuss. Something serious, he said. I was surprised that he wanted to confide in me – we've never been particularly close. Christmas, birthdays, that sort of thing. We arranged to meet at the cottage at seven. That's when I…' Her voice tailed off and she dabbed her eyes with the handkerchief again. 'Well, you know.'

'Did he say what he wanted to talk to you about?' asked Ronald.

'Not in as many words but I got the impression that it might have been about his job. I think he was unhappy at work. He had been for a while, I think, but he would not tell me why.'

'Exactly how much did you know about what he did, Rachel?' asked Blizzard.

'I'd always assumed it was undercover work because of the way he kept disappearing for weeks on end, but I don't think even Polly was terribly sure exactly what he did, and he never told her. I guess he couldn't really.'

The detectives nodded.

'I did see him in a city centre pub one night,' continued Rachel. 'All scruffy with a beard and drinking with a couple of rough-looking men. He blanked me, so I assumed he did not want to be acknowledged. I asked him about it the next time I saw him, but he clammed up. I take it he was undercover for a long time?'

'Ten years, yes,' said Blizzard. 'Came out about a year ago.'

'I guessed he'd stopped.' She noticed the detectives exchange looks. 'Don't look so worried. It's nothing sinister. I worked it out because he seemed to be keeping more regular hours. Even turned up to my son's birthday party. I wondered if that was why he wanted to talk to me tonight. The last time I saw him – just before Christmas when he dropped Jake's present off – he said that he was finding life a bit tame.'

'Tame?' said Blizzard. 'Did he say that?'

'That was the impression he gave. Do you think that he was attacked because of his job, Chief Inspector?'

'It's certainly one of the lines of inquiry that we will be pursuing,' said Blizzard, choosing his words carefully. 'Among many others. Can you think of anyone who would want to harm him? Someone in his private life, maybe?'

'Not really but then his private life was just that. Nothing would surprise me.'

'Did he have a girlfriend?' asked Ronald.

'No, he's still in love with Polly. When I saw him at Christmas, he said he was thinking of finding her and the little one. Try to patch things up.'

'He said the same thing to me this afternoon,' said Blizzard. 'We found an overnight bag at the house. Could he have suddenly decided to go and find them? When I was with him, I got the distinct impression that he'd made his mind up to quit the job.'

'I don't know. I just wish I could be more helpful.' Rachel looked intently at the detectives. 'Can I ask you a question?'

'Sure,' said Blizzard.

'Are you not worried?'

'Worried?'

'Yes. You both worked with Alex so presumably you've got plenty of the same enemies. Are you not worried that whoever tried to kill my brother will come after you?'

Blizzard glanced at Ronald but did not say anything. For the second time in an hour he felt that he did not need to.

* * *

The car made its way through the heavy evening traffic on the bypass, heading past the derelict shipyards and dilapidated former warehouses strung out along the River Haft until it reached the east side of the city with its rundown back streets, deserted trading estates and factories defaced with graffiti, each one a bleak sign that the city was still suffering from the effects of recessions that had ripped the heart out of its heavy industry in the previous decades.

Noting the increased number of police patrol cars on the roads, the driver kept glancing down nervously at the passenger seat where the gun was now concealed beneath a tattered blanket. After twenty minutes, and with some relief, he turned off the busy bypass and guided his vehicle along the quieter road running through the heart of the eastern district. As he came to the edge of the city and the traffic became lighter, he reached a large white mock Tudor roadside pub. The man pulled into the car park of The Swan, cut the engine, reached out to touch the handgun for reassurance and settled down to wait.

* * *

'I take it your governor won't deign to come and see me himself?' asked Detective Inspector Andy Barratt, staring hard at Colley across his desk. 'Too frit?'

'Come on, Andy, behave yourself,' said the sergeant. 'When did you ever see John Blizzard duck out of something? However, he does realise that he's not exactly flavour of the month with you.'

'He's certainly not,' grunted Barratt.

It was shortly after 9pm and the two men were sitting at a table in the deserted Special Operations Squad Room on the fourth floor of force headquarters in the centre of Hafton.

'He was out of order,' continued Barratt. He reached for his mug of tea. 'Made me look foolish in front of the Brass. Cost me a promotion.'

'Time to let it go, Andy. Besides, I'm not sure he *was* out of order. Oh, don't look like that. You know what happened.'

'Blizzard stuck his neb in, that's what happened. Interfering where he wasn't wanted.'

'That's not how it happened and you know it. Alex Mather stumbled across information about one of our inquiries and when Blizzard met him, he realised that he was on the edge so suggested he come out. What alternative did he have? Your lot didn't have a bloody clue. You'd have been happy to leave him there.'

'You always have stood by your governor.'

'He's a good cop, Andy, one of the best and you know it,' said Colley, bridling at the comment. 'That's why I stand by him. Anyway, I don't think that now is the time to discuss this, given that one of our own is in hospital fighting for his life, do you?'

Barratt shook his head.

'No, you're right,' he said, his tone softening. 'How is Alex? Pretty bad, from what I hear. Bullet in the chest, someone said.'

Colley nodded.

'So, what do you need from me?' asked Barratt.

'A list of who might want Alex dead.'

'Where do you want to begin?' said Barratt. He walked over to the filing cabinet in the corner of the room, slid open the top drawer and flicked through the files. 'This is full of people who would be glad to see the back of Alex Mather.'

'I don't suppose there's a file marked Gunmen For Hire, by any chance?'

'You reckon it's a professional hit then?'

'Blizzard thinks it might be. I'm not so sure. You ever known a pro to slug his victim at point blank and leave him alive? Then miss with a second bullet for good measure?'

'Not sure that I have,' said Barratt. He carried a clutch of brown files over to dump them on the desk. 'These contain a dozen names, each with a good reason to wish Alex harm. There's plenty more where they came from and that's not counting the information Alex provided for your governor's sex ring inquiry.'

Colley tried to look undisturbed by the comment.

'Fair enough,' he said.

'I never did understand that,' said Barratt. He sat down and began to leaf through the files. 'One minute, Alex is investigating a couple of low-life pimps on the Ellmead Estate for Vice, the next thing we know he's coming up with chapter and verse on a child sex ring that most people did not believe existed – and which nobody had asked him to investigate. Go figure.'

'I guess he stumbled on all sorts in his line of work.'

'Yeah, but I always wondered if there was more to it than that,' said Barratt with a frown. 'Alex never fully explained it, did his dark and moody act whenever I asked.'

'You know Alex. Ask him the time of day and he thinks twice about telling you.'

'Nevertheless, something did not add up. Blizzard ever say anything about it? It was his inquiry, after all.'

'He always reckoned that Alex got lucky. One of his informants let something slip and the pieces started to fall into place.'

'Well, however he did it, you should definitely include the guys who got locked up from that investigation. From what I hear, there were plenty of threats flying around at the time.'

'Blizzard always reckoned it was hot air.' Colley gestured to the files. 'Any of these stand out? Any of them got a particular reason to dislike Alex?'

'Plenty.' Barratt gave a slight smile. 'I remember the meeting before he went undercover. Vice had some photos pinned on a board. Their top ten targets, they said. Do what you can. Alex said he'd get the lot of them. He'd helped get them all banged up by the time he finished. Well, nine of them anyway.'

'Who's the one that got away?'

'Ah, well, you'll like this,' grinned Barratt. He flicked through the files and opened one to reveal a photograph of a greasy-haired man with a sallow complexion and bad teeth. 'The one who always manages to get away.'

'Eddie Gayle as I live and breathe,' said Colley, looking at the picture.

'Your governor's best mate,' said Barratt. 'Alex always said that Gayle was the one he really wanted because it would make Blizzard's day. Just couldn't do it, though. Really rankled with him.'

'Rankles with us all, Andy. Every time we think we're getting close to him, he slimes his way out of it. One step ahead of us all the time.'

'I know how you feel. Alex told Vice that he was using some of his east-side houses as brothels. Girls from Thailand and Vietnam. All illegals, of course. Trouble was, when they went in, there was no one there and nothing to link Gayle to anything. Nothing strong enough for court, anyway. Alex was livid.'

'Someone tipped Gayle off, you reckon?'

'I do hope not.'

'Yeah, so do I.' Colley drained his mug, stood up and gestured at the files. 'Listen, I hate to be a pain, Andy, but I've got a load to sort back at Abbey Road – any chance that you can email me over a full list of those names?'

'Yeah, sure,' said Barratt, adding as Colley reached the door, 'oh, and Dave?'

Colley turned back into the room.

'Tell your governor he's welcome to drop in for a cuppa if he wants to,' said Barratt. 'Tell him it's been too long. This thing with Alex, it's… well, you know, just tell him, will you?'

'Will do,' said Colley and disappeared into the corridor. 'He'd like that.'

* * *

Shortly after 9pm, a fight broke out in the main bar of The Swan between two men whose argument over a woman turned violent as they fell upon each other with flailing fists and angry shouts. For a few moments, they struggled on the floor then one of them staggered to his feet, blood pouring from a cut lip, and grabbed a bottle which he smashed on the bar before brandishing it furiously at his assailant.

Terrified drinkers scattered and headed for the door, all apart from one craggy-faced man who sat in one of the corner booths, taking no notice of events happening around him, calmly drinking from his pint of beer and doing the crossword in his newspaper. He only looked up when the brawling men came within a few feet of the table.

'For fuck's sake, give over, will you?' murmured Max Randall irritably when one of the men knocked the table and spilled his beer.

The brawl moved away and after a couple of minutes, and with the sound of distant sirens wailing on the night air, spilled out into the car park, where it continued, watched by some of the braver locals.

Sitting in his car thirty feet away, the man with the gun watched the scuffle for a few moments, heard the sirens, slipped the weapon back into the glove compartment and turned the key in the ignition. By the time the first patrol had arrived on the scene and uniformed officers were breaking up the brawling drinkers, the man's car was long since gone, back on the eastern bypass and heading in the direction of the city centre, leaving Max Randall to finish his crossword in peace, while the bar staff began to sweep up the glass and straighten up the furniture.

Chapter five

Blizzard walked into the lounge of The Swan shortly after ten-fifteen and wrinkled his nose at the sour odour, which reminded him of his early days as a police officer working the east side. The inspector ignored the ugly looks from some of the locals and approached the bar, pausing to look down as his shoes crunched on broken glass.

'You been having a party?' he asked the barman, who did not reply. Blizzard put some coins down on the bar. 'Pint of Smith's, please.'

As the drink was poured, the inspector glanced across at one of the corner booths where sat a hangdog man in his early fifties, hair almost grey, thinning and cut short, eyes deep and dark, his face chiselled and pock-marked, with a five o'clock shadow. He was dressed in an ill-fitting navy black suit with no tie. Blizzard smiled, paid for his drink and walked over to where Max Randall was finishing off his crossword, pencil jammed in the corner of his mouth.

'Now then,' said Blizzard affectionately, putting his pint down on the table and sliding into one of the seats.

'Typical flash west-side boy,' said Max Randall in a voice turned gravelly by years of heavy smoking. He did not look up from his newspaper. 'Arrive after all the action finishes.'

'The glass, I take it?'

'Yeah, couple of locals fell out over a girlie.' Randall grinned, filled in the last clue and finally looked up at his old friend. 'Knocked seven shades out of each other. Uniform have just carted them away.'

'Where's a police officer when you want one?' said Blizzard, taking a sip off his ale. 'I *am* assuming that you did your knight in shining armour act and stepped in to uphold the law of the land?'

'Did I fuck as like. I've got enough knob-heads after my blood without adding a couple of piss artists to the list. Uniform can deal with them.' Randall took a swig of beer. 'Surprised to see you here. Thought you'd be up your neck in trouble. How's Alex?'

'He's ...' began the inspector but his voice tailed off as he noticed the suspicious look from one of the men on the next table. Blizzard fixed him with one of his glares. 'You got a problem there, pal?'

The man looked away. It may have been more than twenty years since Blizzard last worked the east side with Max Randall but the DCI's reputation lived on.

'The dirty look,' chuckled Randall, 'is because that's Aidan Horan. You gave him a black eye for lifting some old girl's handbag when you were a rookie plod and he was in short trousers. His father put in an official complaint but no one had seen anything. Funny that.'

'Ah, those were the days,' said Blizzard. He raised his glass at Horan, who noticed the gesture but said nothing.

'Indeed, they were,' said Randall. 'So how *is* Alex? Heard it's touch and go.'

'Bullet near the lung. He's in surgery.'

'Will he live?'

Blizzard shrugged. 'Your guess...' he said.

'Any idea who did it?'

'Too early to say, Max. His cottage hasn't got much in the way of neighbours so no one saw anything and Versace hasn't turned up much, apart from a second bullet. Missed him and stuck in the dresser. Nine mill. The hitman's favourite.'

'Except hitmen don't miss, John, you know that. Whoever did this was not a pro.'

'I guess,' said Blizzard, taking a sip of his beer and grimacing. 'Jesus, that's rank.'

'Stand-in barman. The usual guy got lifted for handling knock-off videos.'

'One of your collars, I take it?'

'Course not,' said Randall. 'Never shit in your own nest, that's what I say. So, what's your thinking on Alex?'

'I've got David Colley drawing up a list of possibles.'

'Hope he's got a big pencil. Alex helped put some heavy-duty crooks away in his time.' Randall lowered his voice. 'Might it be something to do with Keeper? There were enough threats flying around at the time.'

'Yeah, but it was mostly talk.'

'Maybe it was, maybe it wasn't, but you do have an officer with a hole in his chest, do you not? Can I throw a suggestion into the mix? Maybe worth looking at people linked to George Killick.'

'But his death was natural causes, wasn't it?'

'That's the official version.' Randall took another sip of beer and scowled. 'You're right, this is rank. I reckon he knows who we are and pisses in it.'

'I take it you don't buy the official version about Killick?'

'Not really. The cellmate, some no-mark called Roberts, said he only found out he was dead when they woke him up for slopping out but I'm not convinced. Call it instinct. I've got nothing to back it up.'

'But you *are* investigating?'

'Probably putting it a bit strong to say that. More of a box-ticking exercise. My gaffer says he doesn't want me to waste time on it. You know what Phil Glover's like: no imagination, all by the book.'

'Yeah, I know. He and I have had some philosophical discussions on the subject.'

'I bet you have. Phil has not forgiven either of us for freezing him out of the sex ring investigation.'

'Bad feeling or not, though, surely the suspicious death of a prisoner has got to be worth a look?'

'No one mourns the death of a kiddy fiddler, do they?'

'I guess not.'

'Of course, it would all change if there's a link with what happened to Alex,' said Randall. He shot Blizzard a sly look. 'My gaffer would have no option but to let me step things up. Phil Glover couldn't say no if another DCI requested it, could he? Killick had a son. Remember how angry he was when his old man went down?'

Blizzard recalled the lank-haired man striding towards him outside the crown court, hurling profanities, spittle flying from his mouth, his finger jabbing at Blizzard as the threats spewed forth.

'I remember,' said the DCI, 'but it's a big leap from uttering threats in the heat of the moment to planning a cold-blooded murder.'

'Who said it was planned? One of my DCs went to see the son this morning. He was very angry, effing and blinding, saying it was all the police's fault and he'd get even with us. I put it all down to grief but now…'

'There is one problem, though,' said Blizzard. He took another sip of beer and grimaced again. 'Alex did not give evidence against them in order to protect the fact that he had been undercover.'

'Yeah, but everyone knew. Once Alex started turning up on routine inquiries, it was hot news. Let's be honest, we've been waiting for someone to plug him ever since he came out and I've got something that may move Killick's nearest and dearest up the top. An old pal of yours has turned up. One Edward Gayle Esquire.'

'That's more like it,' said Blizzard, leaning forward, his eyes gleaming. 'What's the slimeball got to do with George Killick, though? He never figured in the inquiry.'

'And he's kept well away from the east side since Vice fucked up that raid on his brothel. However, he's been seen over here several times in recent days.'

'Doing what?'

'Dunno, but he's been hanging out with some of our bad lads at that drinking club on River Street.' Randall reached for his glass. 'I didn't think much about it at first – I've got enough on my plate without worrying about a sleaze-bucket like Eddie Gayle – but then I heard that he was seen outside the prison the day before Killick died. Him and his henchman Ronnie Forrester. I did a quick check with my mate the assistant governor. Turns out they'd been to see George Killick twice in the past few days.'

'You think there may be a connection?' asked Blizzard.

'Isn't there always when it comes to Eddie Gayle? There's definitely something going on, anyway. A lot of our informants have gone to ground in recent days and the criminal fraternity have been really edgy. Like they knew something was going to happen. And now Alex gets shot, well, makes you think.'

'OK, tell your governor I want to take a closer look. You and me.'

'Attaboy.' Randall downed his pint, stood up and gestured to the inspector's glass. 'Another one?'

'I'm driving.'

'So am I.' Randall grinned, showing crooked, nicotine-stained teeth. 'I've got this deal with the traffic inspector. He lets me drive home half-cut a couple of nights a week and I don't let on that he's been shagging the arse off the custody sergeant's wife when he's on nights. Not sure that's in the Highway Code. He certainly can't recognise a No Entry sign.'

Blizzard gave a low laugh, downing the remainder of his pint as he stood up.

'You're a disreputable human being, Max,' he said.

As Randall started walking towards the bar, Blizzard reached out to touch his friend softly on the arm. Randall turned round.

'Make sure you watch your back, yeah?' said Blizzard. 'Until we know what's going on, let's be careful.'

'And you be careful, too, old son. The world won't miss another old soak but you've got a little 'un to think about now.'

'I have indeed. One more thing before I go,' said Blizzard, lowering his voice as they walked towards the bar. 'You got any bodies available later tonight if I fancy a few doors kicking in over here? Stir things up a bit.'

'Wouldn't have anything to do with the fact that the chief is after you over your crappy crime stats, would it?' asked Randall, with a mischievous look. 'No matter if it does. I'll always drink to a Blizzard Special. Mind, I'll drink to anything.'

* * *

'He's got to be pissed, this time of night,' said Sergeant Mel Powell, guiding the patrol car along the main road near Abbey Road Police Station and noting the brake lights glow red on the saloon car ahead of him. 'That's three times he's slowed down for no reason.'

'Yeah, let's give him a pull,' said Constable Jane Riley, sitting in the passenger seat.

Powell flicked the blue lights on and closed up on the car. The saloon pulled over to the side of the road. Powell cut the engine and got out of the patrol car.

'Need a hand?' asked the constable.

'Na, I've got it,' said the sergeant, walked up to the driver's side of the saloon and tapped on the window. 'Can I have a word, please, sir?'

Nothing happened for a moment or two then the driver slowly wound down his window and the sergeant found himself staring down the barrel of a handgun.

'Jesus!' he gasped and staggered back.

Seeing his colleague's reaction, Jane Riley leapt from the patrol car and sprinted towards the saloon. As she arrived, a masked man emerged from the driver's side and pointed the weapon at her.

'Stay back!' rasped the gunman.

'Come on, pal,' said the constable, holding up her hands in surrender and noticing with alarm. 'Don't do anything stupid.'

'Who said it would be stupid?' said the man. He turned a trembling hand to train the gun on Powell, who cried out and started to run across the road towards the semi-detached houses.

The gunman aimed and pulled the trigger but the bullet whistled past the sergeant's ear to embed itself into a nearby gate with a dull thud. Powell screamed and threw himself over a low garden wall. Lights went on in nearby houses and one or two curtains twitched. The gunman hesitated, still pointing the weapon in the sergeant's direction, but when the officer did not re-appear from behind the wall, and a man yelled at the gunman from an upstairs bedroom window, he seemed to take fright, clambered into his vehicle and drove off at speed, clipping a couple of parked vehicles before disappearing into the warren of side streets.

A shaking Powell emerged from behind the wall and Jane Riley walked over to stand next to him. The officers watched the car go, waiting for their hearts to stop pounding.

'He didn't look pissed to me,' said Riley when she eventually felt calm enough.

Five minutes later the night air above Hafton was filled with the wail of sirens.

Chapter six

By the time we got ourselves into gear, Alex was out of surgery. Arthur was still at the hospital but no one could give him a straight answer about his chances of survival. The doctors just kept talking about the next twenty-four hours being crucial, like they always do, but Arthur said that he had the impression they weren't telling him the whole story.

Then, of course, we had the incident on Waterson Lane, which only served to heighten tension. The thought that we could have had two officers shot within hours of each other really shook people up. It was turning into one of those nights when something is in the air and anything is possible but none of it good. And it was not even eleven; the night was nowhere near over yet. Which is what allowed me to make my mind up about the raids – wrest back the initiative, hit the villains hard, a Blizzard Special. Make people forget about the bad crime stats? Yeah, maybe that as well.

Blizzard stood at his office window, mug of tea cradled in his hand, and stared out over the Abbey Road car park, deep in thought. These snatched few moments were the first opportunity he had had since the shooting of Alex Mather to think about the events of the last few hours. They were dark thoughts. Like many officers, John

Blizzard had been threatened with a gun before but he'd always got away with it. Now his friend was lying gravely ill in hospital and the inspector was confronting the very real possibility that he might die. Mather would not be the first officer with whom Blizzard had served to die on duty but he would be the first that the inspector counted as a friend.

Randall's words came back to him. *The world won't miss another old soak but you've got a little 'un to think about now.* Blizzard thought of his son and of Fee and wondered, not for the first time since the baby had been born, if the time had come to seek a new job. A light knock on the door disturbed his reverie. He turned to see Colley.

'Any news?' asked the inspector.

'Nope. Uniform have got roadblocks up but nothing's turned up. Mel and Jane are ready to talk. They're in the canteen.'

'Any news on Alex?'

Colley shook his head.

'I guess no news is good news then,' said Blizzard.

'You keep telling yourself that,' replied the sergeant.

* * *

Ronnie Forrester sat in the corner booth of the back-street pub and dialled a number on his mobile. A well-built, shaven-headed man, with tattooed arms and a bulging neck, he was drinking alone, a half-empty pint glass on the table in front of him. No one drank with Eddie Gayle's right-hand man unless they had to. Too scary, they would say when they knew he could not hear them. Too much like bad news even for the men who inhabited Hafton's criminal underworld. Everyone knew what Ronnie Forrester was capable of doing.

The call was answered.

'I just heard,' said Forrester in a low hiss. 'What the fuck were you thinking of? Them uniforms weren't on the list.'

'I panicked,' said the gunman. 'They stopped me and had to get away.'

'And The Swan? What the fuck happened there? Apparently, he's still alive.'

'I waited outside but then there was a fight in the pub and the police turned up so I couldn't do it.'

'If you fuck this up…' hissed Forrester before ending the call.

* * *

'And you've got no idea who he was or why he reacted the way he did?' asked Blizzard, who was sitting next to Colley at one of the tables in the largely empty canteen at Abbey Road and looking across at Powell and Riley. They both still looked pale.

'It was just a routine stop, John,' said Powell. 'Routine as they come. No different to any other.'

Riley nodded.

'Mel's right,' she said. 'Next thing I know the guy is out of the car and shooting at Mel.'

'No indication why?' asked Blizzard.

'Nothing,' said Powell.

'No warnings?'

'None at all.'

'And you didn't recognise him?'

The uniformed officers shook their heads. Blizzard looked at Colley, who was working his way through a bacon sandwich.

'Got to be the same man as hit Alex,' said the inspector. 'Too much of a coincidence, surely? Can't see two guys running round shooting at coppers, can you?'

'Not really,' said Colley. He wiped his lips with a napkin and reached for his mug of tea. 'Ballistics are trying to match the bullets now but Versace says that it's definitely another nine mill.'

'I'm not so sure it was the same man, sir,' said Jane Riley respectfully; everyone knew that it could go either way if you challenged Blizzard. 'Something doesn't seem right.'

The inspector did not seem to mind the comment.

'Why?' he asked.

'Well, everyone is saying that what happened to DC Mather was a hit.' She looked at Blizzard, who gave a slight nod. 'But this guy, he didn't look like the kind of man to do that. His hand was shaking really badly and he missed Mel by quite a bit. It's like he wasn't really used to handling weapons.'

'Now you tell me,' grunted Powell.

'Aye,' said Colley, 'if he was a pro, he'd have finished you off good and proper. Even if he had missed with his first shot, he'd have slugged you over the wall. You'd be pushing up the daisies by now, sunbeam.'

'Yes, thank you for those reassuring words,' said the sergeant. 'Makes me feel much better, that does.'

Colley grinned and took a bite of sandwich.

'However, it does probably strengthen the idea that it is the same man,' said Blizzard. Noticing Riley's questioning expression, he said: 'Whoever shot Alex missed as well. Looks like you're right that he doesn't know guns, Constable.'

Once the uniformed officers had left the canteen, the inspector looked at his sergeant, who had finished his sandwich and was unwrapping a chocolate bar.

'I can't work out if this is good or bad,' said the inspector.

'Struggling to see the good bit,' replied Colley, taking a bite. 'All sounds bad to me. Bad as it comes.'

'Maybe not. See, I'm coming round to your way of thinking. That what we've got on our hands is a lunatic with a personal grudge against the police.'

'Oh, that sort of good,' said Colley, through a mouthful of chocolate. 'Now I understand. I guess that's why you are a DCI and I am just a lowly sergeant. They call it thinking out of the box, I believe.'

'Think about it, though. If it's not a pro who targeted Alex, it's nothing to do with Keeper or anything else Alex was involved in. The guy in Waterston Lane had plenty of opportunity to get away but he seemed determined to take a copper with him. Mel just happened to be in the way,' said Blizzard.

'Ah, but whoever shot Alex went to a lot of trouble to find him. You've been there, you don't go down that lane unless it's for a specific reason.'

'Maybe our guy simply waited outside the station, worked out Alex was a copper and followed him home.'

'Andy Barratt will be hacked off after I asked him to put together the list of heavy criminals,' Colley said.

'You see him?'

'Yeah, he said you'd be welcome to drop in for a cuppa. Think he wants to build some bridges.'

'And why would he do that?'

'Call it my natural charm. He's emailed the list over.' Colley fished a computer print-out from his jacket pocket, straightened it out and slid it across the table towards the inspector. 'A veritable who's who of Hafton villainy, that is.'

'So, it is,' said Blizzard, scanning the names. 'Anyone stand out?'

'They all had reason to dislike Alex but there's nothing specific. Don't know if you've got to the bottom yet but Eddie Gayle is mentioned.'

'Yeah, Max Randall mentioned him as well.' Blizzard slid the list back across the table. 'He also suggested George Killick's family.'

'They've certainly got motive. You want to target them first?' The sergeant gestured to the list. 'We need to slim that little lot down anyway. Can't hit them all.'

'Can't we?' said Blizzard thoughtfully. He tapped the piece of paper. 'Why not hit them all? Tonight.'

'All of them?' Colley looked down at the print-out in amazement. 'But there's loads of the buggers. And these aren't any old common or garden villains, guv, they're all top notch.'

'No one's untouchable.'

'Yes, I know but if we've decided the gunman is not a pro, can we really justify…?'

'We've been saying that we need to make a statement, maybe this is the ideal opportunity. The last thing the crooks want is a load of heat coming down on their heads. They may well give up our shooter just to get rid of us. Wouldn't be the first time that's happened and someone will know who he is.'

A uniformed officer walked into the canteen.

'The gunman's car?' he said. 'It's turned up on the wasteland behind the shops on Fenby Avenue. Torched. Versace's guys are on their way out there but my guys reckon there's not much left to go on.'

'No idea what he's driving now?'

'There's eight been nicked tonight. We've got alerts out on them all but nothing so far. Nothing at our roadblocks. There's got to be a good chance that he's away.'

'That settles it then,' said Blizzard, standing up with a scrape of chair legs. 'Let's go for it.'

'Jesus,' breathed Colley, his eyes bright. 'A strike against the top city villains all in one go. Hafton will have seen nothing like it. There'll be hell on.'

'Which is exactly why we do it.'

'Happy days are here again,' said Colley. He finished his chocolate bar and followed the inspector from the room, scrunching up his wrapper and drop-kicking it into the bin as he did so. 'Get in!'

* * *

It was just after eleven when the weary surgeon approached Arthur Ronald and Rachel Mather in the largely empty third floor waiting room.

'How is he?' asked Rachel anxiously, getting to her feet.

'Not good, I am afraid,' said the surgeon. 'We nearly lost him twice. He was improving slightly when we finished but he could easily take a turn for the worst. The damage to the area around his lung is extremely severe. It really is minute by minute.'

'What are his chances?' asked Ronald.

'I learnt a long time ago not to answer that question when it comes to gunshot injuries, Superintendent,' said the surgeon. He looked at Rachel. 'And even if he does pull through, it will be a long road to recovery. He'll need a lot of support. You have to start thinking about that.'

'We'll look after him,' said Rachel. 'Can we see him?'

The surgeon nodded and led them down the corridor to the intensive care unit where Alex Mather lay connected to an array of tubes and beeping monitors.

'He looks so peaceful,' said Rachel quietly, looking at the surgeon. 'Just like he's asleep.'

'He may well look peaceful but beneath the surface there's a battle royal under way.' The surgeon looked at Ronald. 'We got the bullet out. I assume that you will want it for your forensics people to examine?'

Ronald was about to reply when his mobile phone rang.

'I do apologise,' he said as a couple of the nurses frowned at him. He walked into the corridor and took the call.

'Blizzard,' said a voice.

'Please tell me that you have got the man who fired at our people.'

'I am afraid not, Arthur, but I've had an idea…'

Chapter seven

'Thank you for coming in at such short notice,' said Blizzard, looking round the room 'We want to strike hard and quickly and I know that none of you would want to miss out.'

It was shortly before midnight and a large team of uniformed and plainclothes officers sat in the briefing room at Abbey Road Police Station, each one looking towards John Blizzard, who was pacing about in front of them. There was a feeling of expectation; Blizzard's briefings were legendary and everyone eagerly awaited his next words as they surveyed the row of mugshots pinned on the board.

'This little lot of lovelies,' said Blizzard, 'will be familiar to many of you. It is a salutary thought that each of us could fill our own boards with faces like these. We have all made enemies through the job and I do not want the city's criminals thinking that they can get away with what happened tonight.'

The inspector stopped pacing and sought out Powell and Riley, who were sitting together having dismissed the suggestion that they take the rest of the shift off to recover from their ordeal.

'Tonight is unprecedented in its scale,' said Blizzard. He let his gaze roam round the room, one of his favourite tricks in briefings, a call to arms for each officer. 'But what happened tonight was an attack on every one of us – just ask Mel – and I want the criminals to know that this division is ours.'

A murmur of agreement rippled round the room and there was a smattering of applause. Blizzard was old school, an officer whose support of community policing only went so far, and the officers loved him for it. It was the approach that had allowed he and Ronald to oversee such dramatic reductions in crime and everyone had been wondering how they would react to the disappointing statistics. The gleam in Blizzard's eye gave them their answer.

'Each one of these men is of interest,' said Blizzard, tapping the board, 'because they went to jail, in part, because of evidence that Alex provided. And they are not the only ones. David could have filled the board three times over.'

Blizzard looked at Colley, who was in his usual position leaning against the wall at the back of the room.

The sergeant nodded.

'Easily,' he said. 'I don't imagine Alex Mather gets many cards at Christmas.'

Another low ripple of laughter ran round the room.

'Are some of these guys not still in prison?' asked a uniformed officer. She pointed to the picture of a squab-nosed man. 'Billy Knott certainly is. I arrested him myself.'

'Indeed he is,' said Blizzard, 'and where they are locked up, we have identified key associates for a visit. We didn't want them to miss out. We're a big believer in equality in Western Division.'

Some of the officers laughed again. Before Blizzard could continue, Arthur Ronald lumbered into the room.

Noticing all eyes turned towards him, the superintendent took a seat at the back and shook his head wearily.

'Sorry,' he said. 'No change but I'll tell you something for free, he's a fighter is our Alex. Carry on, John, don't mind me. I take it you're doing one of your ra-ra specials? You need me to get the pom-poms out of the play cupboard?'

'No, I'm fine,' said Blizzard with a smile. He looked out across the assembled officers. 'OK, any other questions so far?'

'Yes,' said a detective. 'I don't want to be funny, guv – I like the idea of kicking in doors as much as the next man – but where are we going to put them all? Should we not be narrowing the list down a bit?'

Blizzard looked at the speaker, a slim man with short-cropped brown hair, an angular face, a prominent nose and a thin mouth. It was the question he expected from the man he expected it from. Chris Ramsey was one of the Division's detective inspectors: the organiser, the one who worried about the practicalities. Although Blizzard had long regarded Ramsey as lacking imagination as a result, he had come to rely heavily on him and afforded the detective respect.

'You're right, of course,' said the DCI. 'Central are going to give up some cells but we do need to prioritise.'

'How many of them did Alex actually give evidence against?' asked Ramsey. 'He never testified in court during his ten years undercover, as far as I know.'

'True enough but since he came out, every criminal knows what he did. Until we think otherwise, every crook in this city is a suspect. OK, your senior officers will brief you on your targets. Oh, and remember, no one is untouchable. No one.'

Amid the scraping of chairs and the excited buzz of conversation, the officers headed for the door. Graham Ross approached Blizzard, holding a brown file.

'Versace,' said Blizzard. 'What you got?'

'Not much,' said Ross, holding up the file. 'However, we dug a bullet out of a gatepost in Waterston Lane, the one that missed Mel Powell, and ballistics reckon it's from the same weapon that shot Alex. It's quite an old firearm and has not been used for a long time. There's nothing to link it to any other crimes either. It's looking less and less like a pro.'

After Ross had departed, Blizzard stood for a few moments in the largely deserted briefing room. Arthur Ronald, who had remained seated, walked over to him.

'You sure about this?' asked the superintendent quietly. He nodded at the mugshots on the wall. 'We've not got much on any of them. We could end up looking stupid if it goes wrong. Won't do anything to help my ulcer.'

'Didn't know you had an ulcer.'

'I'm thinking of getting one.'

Blizzard looked affectionately at his friend.

'Relax,' he said. 'We'll be OK. Besides, we have got to be seen to be doing something. And it's too late to call it off, I've told the canteen we're going to need a hundred and fifty bacon sandwiches.'

'Yes, but the chief needed a lot of convincing that it is not a knee-jerk reaction. Reckons you're using it to deflect attention from the crime stats. If we don't turn up anything…'

'Turn over stones in this city and something will always crawl out. You know that, Arthur. Might not be what you were looking for, but it'll be something. If you've got doubts, think of Alex Mather in his hospital bed.'

Ronald thought for a few moments and nodded.

'Come on,' he said. He slapped his friend on the shoulder. 'Let's wake some low-lifes up.'

'That's more like it,' said Blizzard.

Twenty-five minutes after the inspector finished his briefing, a column of police vans and patrol vehicles snaked its way out of the station yard onto deserted night-time streets before dispersing to raid homes on the housing estates and terraced streets strung across the western side of the city.

* * *

Five miles away, Max Randall was leaning against a wall in the yard behind one of the east-side police stations, smoking a cigarette and watching uniformed officers loading their equipment into a series of vans. A sergeant in full riot gear walked over, with a sceptical look on his face. He held up a piece of paper in a gloved hand.

'You sure about this, Max?' he asked. 'Looks like a bit of a fishing exercise by your mate, if you ask me. Are we not just massaging John Blizzard's ego because his crime stats are crap?'

'It doesn't harm to put the message out from time to time,' said Randall. He took another drag on his cigarette and blew smoke out into the crisp night air. 'Besides, we do have an officer lying in a hospital bed fighting for his life, remember. And another who escaped serious injury only because some lunatic can't shoot straight.'

The officer nodded; he had served with Mel Powell when they were together in the traffic division.

'Fair enough, Max,' he said, running his eye down the piece of paper. 'If you're sure. Three addresses, yeah?'

'Yeah, three,' nodded Randall. 'Oh, and I want us to lift Barrie Killick as well.'

'You're kidding, yeah? I mean it's not twenty-four hours since his old man died.'

'I know but we're lifting him anyway. And watch yourself. He's really worked up after his father's death and he's perfectly capable of turning violent.'

'So am I,' said the sergeant with a grin. He patted the stick hanging from his belt and headed back towards the vans. 'And I've got more friends than him.'

Randall gave a crooked smile, took a final drag on his cigarette, dropped it and ground it into the tarmac with his shoe.

'Sometimes,' he said, heading for his car, 'I love this fucking job.'

Chapter eight

Arthur was right that the raids were a gamble and that we had nothing definite on any of those on the list. However, we had to be seen to be doing something. Anything to reinforce the idea that we still had control of the streets. The crime stats dictated that much. Besides, like I told Arthur, if you turn over enough stones you'd be amazed what crawls out although I'm not sure any of us expected what we discovered at Eddie Gayle's house. Or where it would take us. And we certainly did not expect to find the young lad in Rowan Avenue. Just shows what lives under those stones, doesn't it?

Shortly before midnight, Blizzard and Colley left Abbey Road Police Station in the inspector's car, accompanied by a police van containing a team of uniformed officers in riot gear. After driving for a few minutes through the night-time streets, they found themselves in one of the many tree-lined avenues that criss-crossed the city's affluent western suburbs.

Driving past the large detached houses with their ornate fountains and immaculately-kept lawns, each home worth at least a million, Blizzard frowned as he always did when he visited the area. He knew that, although many of the houses belonged to successful business people, some belonged to criminals and the knowledge had always irked him. Eventually, he pulled up outside a large detached mock Tudor house concealed behind a high wall, got out and peered through the gate.

'Who says crime doesn't pay?' he said.

'You need a new scriptwriter,' said Colley, joining him to peruse the darkened house at the end of the drive. 'You say that every time we come here. You reckon Eddie is in?'

'Who cares?' said the inspector, looking over to one of the uniformed officers who had climbed out of the van. 'You got the warrant?'

The officer smiled and held up a hydraulic ram.

'Sure have,' he said. 'You want me to break in?'

'It would seem rude not to,' said Blizzard.

'Eddie will be livid when he finds out what you've done,' said Colley. 'You know what his lawyer's like. He'll put in an official complaint, for sure, and the chief did say we had to be careful after the last time. Harassment and all that.'

'Yeah, perhaps I need to think a bit more carefully about this.' Blizzard nodded at the uniformed officer. 'OK, done that now. Go for it.'

Colley shook his head but there was a slight smile on his face and the detectives watched as the uniformed officer smashed his way through the gate. The vehicles edged their way into the drive, pulling up outside the house, wheels crunching on the gravel as they drew to a halt.

'And again,' said Blizzard, getting out the vehicle and ringing on the doorbell but not waiting for a reply.

'I take it you are going to take the flak for this?' said the uniform. 'Two boys on Traffic came close to losing their jobs last month just because they did not follow the right procedure in pulling Gayle over. Word was it was only when the Fed rep threatened to sue that the chief backed down. He was all for sacking them on the spot.'

'Typical,' snorted Blizzard.

'And smashing down Eddie Gayle's front door is big stuff,' continued the uniformed officer. 'His lawyer is bound to kick off again.'

'You just leave Eddie and his weasily lawyer to me,' said Blizzard. 'I'll tell the chief all this was done on my say-so. Senior officer and all that.'

The uniform nodded – he knew that Blizzard would be as good as his word – and smashed down the door. Blizzard led the way into the house and, while uniformed officers searched upstairs, he and Colley walked around the downstairs rooms, flicking on the lights as they went and staring at the gaudy ornaments and garish paintings.

'You know,' said Colley as he joined Blizzard in the spacious living room with its plush bright green swirled carpet and large gold-framed mirror running the length of much of one wall, 'every time I come here, I can't help thinking that, if nothing else, Eddie Gayle is guilty of crimes against good taste. Perhaps we should call in the Fashion Police.'

'Or Versace.'

Colley chuckled; a Blizzard joke was a rare thing and to be appreciated.

'Anyway, that's the least of his crimes,' said Blizzard. He sat down on the leather sofa and stared at the large television at the far end of the room. 'Hey, that's massive.'

'They're new,' said Colley, eying it with admiration. 'Came out just before Christmas. Neat piece of kit, an all-in entertainment system without all that faffing about with different remotes. Perhaps Eddie's an Angry Birds fan.'

Blizzard looked bewildered.

'Sorry,' said Colley, 'forgot you've only just discovered black and white telly. Anyway, suffice to say they don't come cheap. I was looking at them in the shop the other day but they're well beyond a humble sergeant's wage.'

'Better go for that inspector's job then.'

'No thanks,' said Colley. He walked over to the set and ran a finger slowly across the top. 'Jay says it would make me miserable.'

'Wise woman is your missus.'

'She is indeed. And I'd miss your beaming face of a morning.' The sergeant looked round the room. 'Our Eddie has clearly been raking it in and I'm not sure all this came from his activities as a rogue landlord.'

'Agreed.' Blizzard began prowling round the room, opening cupboards and drawers. 'But is he the type to organise a hit on Alex?'

'Say what you like about Eddie but he's not stupid. No one has ever dared give evidence against him so he has no reason to bump off a copper.'

'Maybe.' The inspector tried a drawer in the bureau and found it locked. Looking round, he spied a letter opener and used it to force his way in. Pulling out the drawer, he found a pile of papers, on the top of which was a page torn from a notebook. He gave a low whistle. 'Or maybe not.'

'What you got?' asked the sergeant walking over to him.

Blizzard looked closer at the scribbled numbers, then held the paper up so that the sergeant could see.

'You recognise that number?' he asked.

'That's Alex's mobile, I think.' The sergeant took his mobile phone out of his coat pocket and scrolled down his contacts list. 'Yes, that's him alright.'

'Now why would Eddie Gayle have Alex Mather's number?'

'And how did he get hold of it in the first place?' asked Colley. 'Took me six months to wheedle it out of the bugger. Do we assume that he knows where Alex lives as well?'

'If he does, that takes Eddie Gayle to the top of our list,' said Blizzard with a gleam in his eye. 'Alex has been passing information through on him for years, including that botched Vice Squad raid on his brothel. Maybe Eddie worked out what he had been doing and decided it was payback time.'

'What's more, the techies reckon Alex received a call from Number Unknown just before he was shot. They are having all on to trace it back. Maybe it was Eddie Gayle, checking he was in so he could send his hitman.'

Blizzard pursed his lips.

'No one would like to collar Eddie Gayle more than me,' he said, 'but it all sounds too good to be true. You're right, Eddie may be a sleaze-ball but he's not a stupid sleaze-ball. He knows that trying to top a police officer changes everything. They all know that.'

'So, maybe talk of big-time villains is wrong,' said the sergeant. He sat down on the leather sofa and wearily closed his eyes. 'Maybe we are looking for someone with a more personal motive.'

'Which takes us back to George Killick's family.' Blizzard looked across to the door as a uniformed sergeant walked into the room. 'Please tell me that you have found a handwritten confession taped to a warm nine millimetre handgun.'

'I am afraid not but none of the beds have been slept in. If you ask me, your man's done a runner. My gaffer's just been on. They need help on one of the other raids. Gayle's pal Ronnie Forrester. He was not at the address we were given but they know where he is. Can you spare us?'

'Yes, we'll hang round here a bit,' said Blizzard. 'Just watch Forrester, he's an evil bastard.'

'I know all about Ronnie Forrester,' said the uniformed sergeant ruefully. 'Damn near broke my arm the last time I arrested him. Been waiting for another go.'

The detectives went outside and watched the van pull off the drive. When it had gone, the officers went to sit in the inspector's car where they listened on the radio for the next twenty minutes as the division's officers hit the area's crooks and hit them hard. Doors were smashed in, warnings yelled and criminals dragged protesting from their beds before being bundled into vans.

'You think this will achieve anything?' asked Colley as they heard one of the uniformed sergeants reporting another raid. 'I mean, we've hardly taken a scientific approach to this, have we?'

'You sound like the chief.' Blizzard glanced back at the house. 'Eddie's not coming, is he?'

'If the word was out that Alex was going to be shot, maybe he decided to lie low for a while.'

Silence settled on the car for a few moments.

'I never asked how come you hate him so much,' said Colley eventually. 'Keep meaning to. What did he do to hack you off so badly?'

The inspector hesitated as if gathering his thoughts.

'I've seen a lot of death in my time, David,' he said. 'Too much. Most of it just washes over me but sometimes one gets through the defences.'

'Been there. What happened?'

'It was just after I'd come to work in Western. I'd been at CID on the east side with Max Randall but a sergeant's posting came up in the Drugs Squad at Abbey Road and Max suggested I go for it.' Blizzard smiled. 'Nothing to do with a sergeant's job coming up on the east side which I was likely to get ahead of him, of course. Arthur was already over here as a detective inspector so he put a word in.'

'That's when you met Eddie Gayle?'

Blizzard nodded and shifted in his seat to ease the nagging pain in his chronically bad back, which always played up when the weather was cold.

'I'd been aware of him on the east side, everyone was aware of Eddie Gayle on the east side, but I'd never met him. That happened on my second day in Drugs at Abbey Road. Uniform got a call to one of Eddie's bedsits, real shit-hole it was. Typical Eddie Gayle. One of the residents was worried about her friend. Uniform broke into the kid's room and found her dead with a needle sticking out of her arm. Heroin overdose.'

'And you got called in?'

'Because of the drugs link.' Blizzard hesitated. He shook his head. 'She looked so young lying on the bed, David, she really did. I'd seen death before, of course I had, but something about this kid… how young she was… the reaction of her parents, it really got to me. Then Mum killed herself six weeks later. Fell in front of a train at Hall Lane railway station. The coroner said he couldn't be sure it wasn't an accident but I knew…'

His voice tailed off. Colley said nothing; the sergeant had noticed that a more emotional side to John Blizzard had been emerging since the birth of his son. Colley had experienced similar sensations himself when his daughter was born. Blizzard had always said that officers who became parents found that the emotions they experienced made the job harder to do. Colley had never agreed, he had always thought that the arrival of Laura had made him a better person and a better police officer, but he knew why the inspector had long held the view. It was a question of perspective. Emotions made you more aware of victims but also made you vulnerable.

'Anyway,' said Blizzard eventually, 'it turned out the kid had been behind on her rent. Eddie Gayle sent one of his heavies round to give her a warning the night before she died. He chose Ronnie Forrester. Nasty piece of work. Seventeen and they do that to her. The pathologist reckoned she took an overdose to quell the pain.'

'Did you nick Eddie?' asked Colley, reaching down to adjust the radio as it started hissing. Within seconds, the voices of the officers supervising the raids could be heard clearly again.

'Na. Same old, same old. No one prepared to talk, no chance of getting a charge past the lawyers. All Eddie was interested in was when he could rent the room out again. I vowed then that, however long it took me, I'd get him.

Him and that bastard Forrester. Never thought that I'd still be waiting all these years later.'

'You'll get him one day.'

'Yes, but not, I suspect, over this.'

A burst of conversation on the radio heralded another spate of activity as one of the teams secured their target. Blizzard switched on the car's ignition.

'Come on,' said the inspector. 'We're wasting our time here. Let's get back to Abbey Road, see what low-lifes the cat's dragged in. Second thoughts, let's go and see Ronnie Forrester first.'

Colley looked at the house with the front door swinging forlornly on one hinge.

'What we going to do about that?' he said. 'Shouldn't we have got uniform to stay watching the place in case it gets screwed over?'

'Silly me,' said the inspector guiding the car down the drive. 'I knew I'd forgotten something.'

'You are a wicked man, John Blizzard.'

'And don't you forget it.'

'But I am here to save you from yourself,' said the sergeant. 'If the house does get done over, you'll be in the biggest trouble you've ever been in.'

'I suppose you're right,' sighed the inspector, unclipping the radio handset. 'Pity, though.'

* * *

The door to the plush detached house in Rowan Avenue offered no resistance to the hydraulic ram and the uniformed officers poured into the darkened hallway amid much hollering. A number of them clattered up the stairs and, while two officers burst into the front bedroom, roughly shaking from sleep a middle-aged couple, two more entered the back bedroom, flicking on the light to reveal a young man lying with a girl.

'Police,' said one of the officers, pulling back the covers to reveal that the couple were naked.

The girl screamed as rough hands grabbed her boyfriend and hauled him from the bed.

'What the…?' he spluttered.

A uniformed inspector entered the room and watched as the boy started hurling obscenities at the officers.

'Get him out of here,' said the inspector. His gaze alighted on a chest of drawers, on top of which sat a plastic bag containing a brown substance. The inspector walked over and surveyed it. 'Well, well, what do we have here then? Cannabis, if I am not mistaken.'

The officer glanced down at the floor and saw an open holdall containing several more sealed bags, also containing blocks of brown resin.

'Oh, dear,' he said, looking at the boy. 'I am afraid you are under arrest, sunshine.'

'You don't know who you are messing with,' said the young man.

'If I had a pound for every toerag that has said that to me, I'd be a very rich man indeed. And my last bank statement suggests I'm not. Get your clothes on.'

'Believe me,' said the boy. 'You *really* do not know who you are messing with. No one crosses us.'

As the boy was being taken away, the inspector watched in pensive silence. Something about the way the young man had spoken had disturbed him.

'Hey,' said the inspector as the boy reached the door. 'What's your name, son?'

The boy turned at the door and gave a knowing smile.

'Luke Callaghan,' he said. 'You probably know my grandfather.'

'Not Nathaniel Callaghan?' asked the officer in a flat voice.

'The very same.'

The officer closed his eyes.

'Shit,' he said.

'Listen,' said Luke, walking over to him. 'I'll do you a deal.'

'I don't do deals. Not with the likes of you.'

'You might want to with me. The last thing you want is to be asked why you lifted Nathaniel Callaghan's grandson and the last thing I want is the old man finding out that I've been doing drugs. He's a bit funny about drugs my grandfather.'

'He's a bit funny about a lot of things,' said the officer bleakly.

'Then let me go, pretend you did not find anything and we can both get on with our lives. No one else need know.'

The inspector noted that his colleagues were listening intently and as he surveyed their faces, John Blizzard's final words in the briefing came back to him. *No one is untouchable. No one.*

'Get him out of here,' he said. 'He's someone else's problem now.'

* * *

Ronnie Forrester had just gone to bed when the police officers smashed through the front door of his flat on a housing estate close to Abbey Road Police Station. Having just slipped into an alcohol-infused slumber, it took Forrester a few seconds to react to the shouts and the boots thundering down the hallway. By the time he was fully awake, the officers had burst into his bedroom, the darkness pierced by the head-torches that several of them were wearing.

Someone put on the main light and Forrester could see that there were four of them.

'Ronnie Forrester,' said one of the officers, 'You are under arrest.'

Forrester grabbed for the baseball bat that he kept beside the bed but was too slow and he was dragged to his feet. He gave an enraged roar and snapped out a meaty fist, which brought a pained grunt from one of the police officers. Before Forrester could throw a second punch, the wind was knocked out of him by a baton jabbed hard into his ribs by a female officer and he sunk to his knees, fighting for breath, spittle dripping from his mouth. As he knelt there, pain engulfing his body, he saw a pair of brogues enter the room and walk over to him. Forrester looked up into the face of John Blizzard.

'That was police brutality,' gasped Forrester.

'Reasonable force, Ronnie,' said Blizzard. He looked across at the other officers. 'Get this trash out of here.'

'You've not heard the last of this,' snarled Forrester as he was hauled to his feet by uniformed officers.

'Don't tell me, I'll be hearing from your lawyer.'

'Too right you will,' snarled Forrester as he was led from the room, barging into Colley who was standing in the doorway.

'He's a real charmer, isn't he?' said the sergeant, Forrester's enraged protests fading away as he was led from the flat. Colley glanced over at the uniformed officer who was rubbing his jaw following the blow from Forrester's fist. 'You OK, Mike?'

The officer nodded weakly and Colley glanced at the officer who had struck the blow with the baton.

'You were lucky Megan was here to keep you safe,' said Colley.

She grinned.

Chapter nine

When Blizzard and Colley returned to Abbey Road, the custody area was a hive of activity, crammed with angry men. Some of them were glaring at officers, some were muttering profanities and some were sulky and silent, uneasy at the show of force and determined to give nothing away. Ronnie Forrester sat in a corner, glowering at anyone who glanced in his direction, and not far away Luke Callaghan tried to appear calm but the constant drumming of his foot on the floor belied his nerves.

The arrival of John Blizzard did little to improve the suspects' mood as he stood in the centre of the room and perused them with a broad smile on his face.

'Excellent,' he said, to no-one in particular. 'Hacked off criminals, that's what I like to see.'

For a moment it looked as if Ronnie Forrester was going to be the one to reply but the glint in the inspector's eye changed his mind and he settled for glaring balefully at the detective. Chris Ramsey walked over to Blizzard.

'We get all of them?' asked Blizzard. He nodded at the clipboard in the detective inspector's hand.

'Yeah,' said Ramsey, his lips moving silently as he counted. 'Twenty-one. Nope, tell a lie, twenty-two. All apart from Eddie Gayle. I gather he's slimed his way into the night?'

'He'll turn up. Anything interesting from the searches?'

'Plenty but not what we were looking for, unfortunately.' Ramsey gave a half-smile. 'But tonight was never about that, was it?'

'Not really, but it would have been nice if it had turned up a warm nine mill. And by the sounds of it we did turn up some useful stuff?'

'Can't argue with that.' Ramsey referred to his clipboard again. 'Thirty grand's worth of grade-A heroin, one cannabis farm complete with hydroponics system, a couple of shotguns, one that might have been used in that building society job last month.' He continued running his hand down the page. 'Three machetes. Oh, and a knife we think was used to stab the tom in Laurel Street. And two stolen cars, although neither match the one stopped in Waterston Lane.'

'Good for clear-up rates if nothing else,' said Blizzard. 'That'll keep the chief happy.'

'Not sure this next bit will. See, there's one name that we did not expect. He turned up at the Rowan Avenue address.' Ramsey hesitated. 'And he means trouble.'

'They all mean trouble, Chris.'

'Not like this one. It's Luke Callaghan.'

'Please tell me that the name is a coincidence.'

'As you keep telling us, Blizzard's First Law of Investigation discounts the possibility of coincidence. He's one of Nathaniel's grandsons.'

'Brilliant,' sighed Blizzard. 'That's the last thing we need. What was he doing in Hafton? I thought the Callaghans operated out of Leeds these days.'

'Yeah, they do, but it seems that young Luke has been shagging the target's daughter.' Ramsey gave a slight smile. 'Out of wedlock as well. Not sure how that sits with Nathaniel's religious belief in the sanctity of marriage.'

'Yes, well, be that as it may, it's not a crime, is it? Let's send meladdo on his way and…'

'Ah, were it that simple. See, Luke also had several grand's worth of cannabis in his possession, and when they searched his room they found six hundred quid in notes. Looks like he's been dealing and I am sure I don't have to remind you about the chief's recent edict saying that we are still going to be tough on cannabis. Even turned up being interviewed by Piers Morgan on morning telly, as I recall.'

'Ironically, it's one of the few things I agree with the chief about. And even more ironically, Luke's grandfather would agree, too. He detests drugs, as well you know. What you done with meladdo?'

'He's the long-haired kid in the corner, the one with the earring,' said Ramsey. 'Thought I'd let you make that call, given the circumstances.'

'Not exactly a typical Callaghan, is he?' said Blizzard, surveying the young man with interest. 'We heard from Nathaniel yet?

'The kid used his phone call to ring him. His lawyer is on the way.'

'Then bail him. And do it before the lawyer gets here.'

'Now, hang on,' protested Ramsey. 'Do you not want to at least talk to him first?'

'No, just get him out of my station, Chris. ASAP.'

'But what about all your big speeches about no one being untouchable? That rule not apply to the Callaghans then?'

'You know the situation.' Noticing that several detainees were listening to the conversation, Blizzard lowered his voice. 'We're not even supposed to talk to the buggers. Besides, we're not dropping it. I'll get Arthur to talk to headquarters, see what they want to do. This inquiry is complicated enough without us getting tangled up with the Callaghans unless we really need to.'

'Yes, but…'

'Just leave it, Chris,' hissed Blizzard. Seeing the detective inspector's chastened expression, he softened his tone and reached out to rest a hand on his shoulder. 'Nobody would like more than me than to take on the Callaghans but I'm in enough shit with the chief without going against him on the matter.'

Ramsey nodded gloomily. 'I guess. But I don't like it.'

'None of us like it. How did East do?'

'They're holding three bodies until the morning but Max Randall is bringing Barrie Killick over now. Ah, talk of the devil.'

The detective inspector looked across to where Max Randall was ushering in a man dressed in a T-shirt and tattered jeans. Barrie Killick's eyes flashed fury as he spied Blizzard.

'I might have known you were behind this,' snarled Killick. 'Not enough to hound my father into his grave then?'

'Good to see you too, Barrie,' said Blizzard calmly. He looked at the custody sergeant. 'I want to interview him straight away.'

'God knows where we'll put him afterwards,' said the harassed sergeant, rubbing a hand across his brow. 'Last time we run a two for the price of one offer.'

'Yeah, sorry about that,' smiled Blizzard. He turned to Randall. 'He cause you any bother, Max?'

'Na,' said Randall as Killick glared at the inspector. 'Nice as pie was our Barrie. We had a lovely chat in the car.'

'You want to be in on the interview?'

'Sure do, matey.'

***

Twenty minutes later, Blizzard and Randall were sitting in one of the oppressive little interview rooms, sweating in the fetid heat and looking across the table at Killick and his sallow-faced lawyer, who was eying Blizzard with a knowing look on his face.

'Didn't realise you'd taken up fishing, Chief Inspector,' said the solicitor. 'What was it, arrest anyone with a surname between A and K? I take it this is about the unfortunate events earlier tonight?'

'It is,' said the inspector.

'Yes, well everyone understands that you want to be seen to be doing something but this is over the top. And it's a pretty poor show to arrest a man less than twenty-four hours after the death of his father.'

'We had our reasons.' Blizzard looked at Killick. 'Tell me, Barrie, does the name Alex Mather mean anything to you?'

'No.' The tone of voice was surly, the anger he had displayed in the custody suite replaced by a brooding demeanour. 'Should it?'

'I thought it might, given that he was one of those who helped send your father to prison.'

'Yeah, well I ain't never heard of him.'

'Be that as it may,' said Blizzard, 'Detective Constable Alex Mather was shot and seriously injured late this afternoon. He may yet die and whoever did it could be looking at a murder charge. They throw away the key for anyone who kills a copper. Whoever did it would probably never get out.'

'What's that got to do with me?' Killick's tone was guarded. He looked to his solicitor for reassurance. 'I don't know nothing about this Mather bloke. I never even heard the name.'

'Yes, well I remain to be convinced of that,' said Blizzard. 'And it would not be a mighty leap to assume that you hold Alex Mather responsible for what happened to your father. According to Detective Inspector Randall here, you were uttering all sorts of threats this morning.'

'I was upset but it doesn't mean that I'd be stupid enough to try to kill him. And I never mentioned this Mather bloke anyway.'

'Chief Inspector,' said the lawyer. 'This is unwarranted behaviour. Many officers were involved in the sex ring investigation. Even if my client were so inclined, why would he single out this man Mather? To the best of my recollection, he did not even give evidence at the trial.'

'You've got to start somewhere. Perhaps Alex is not the only officer he is planning to target.'

'I would have expected better of you, Chief Inspector,' said the lawyer. 'You have always been fair with my clients but this is different. You have no grounds on which to accuse my client and you know it.'

Blizzard's face was a mask but he had long since realised how poorly he was coming over in the interview. The lawyer was right.

'So,' said Blizzard, 'if he's innocent, he won't mind telling me where he was between 4.30pm and 7pm.'

'On the road,' said Killick. 'I'm a van driver.'

'Didn't you take the day off because of what happened to your father?' asked Randall.

'Needed the money. I made my last delivery at four in Wakefield.'

'You could still have got back to Hafton.'

'There was an accident on the A1. Lorry went into a bus or summat, not far from the turn-off. I sat in a traffic jam for an hour and a half. Didn't get back until past six. You can check. A.T. Maynards on the Hacton Lane Industrial Estate.'

Blizzard nodded glumly; he had heard a report of the accident on the radio. His expression was not lost on the lawyer.

'It would seem,' said the solicitor calmly, 'that such a thing is relatively easy to check in the morning so in the meantime might I suggest that…?'

'And what about 11pm?' asked Blizzard, cutting across the solicitor. 'When someone shot at two officers in Waterston Lane. Where were you then, Barrie?'

'In bed,' said Killick.

'Tell me about your father,' said Randall, leaning forward. 'Tell me about what happened to him, Barrie.'

'You know what happened,' snarled Killick, the fire back in his eyes. 'You can't tell me the other bloke in the cell didn't hear what happened. He just lay there and let my father die. That's as good as murder, that is. That's what you should be investigating instead of this shit.'

'In which case,' said Randall, 'we would very much like to talk…'

'Might I suggest there are better places to discuss this than here?' said the lawyer. He glanced up at the wall clock and clipped shut his briefcase. He looked at Blizzard. 'Either charge my client or let him go. I've got two more clients in here and I would rather like to get to bed at some stage.'

Blizzard wearily wafted a hand.

'Get him out of my sight,' he said.

When the solicitor and his client had gone, Randall sighed.

'That did not go well,' he said. 'I can't see Killick as the man who shot Alex. I know he made all those threats but, like you said, it's hot air.'

'Yeah, I know,' said Blizzard wearily and stood up to leave the room. As he did so, Colley popped his head round the door.

'Ronnie Forrester's lawyer is here,' he said. 'Want to know who it is?'

Blizzard rolled his eyes. 'I can guess,' he said.

'Should I bring them in?'

Blizzard nodded. 'Go on then.'

As Randall left the room and Colley took his place at the desk, a uniformed officer brought in a scowling Forrester and his solicitor. Paul D'Arcy. No stranger to police attention, he was the lawyer to the city's criminals. A local solicitor who had become immensely, and mysteriously, rich, he was a thin-faced man in his late thirties, dressed immaculately in a dark pinstripe suit with a white handkerchief. He took his seat and shot the inspector a sour look.

'I hope you have a good reason for this circus,' he said.

'I've got an officer fighting for his life, that's all the reason I need.'

'All of which is very regrettable, no one likes to see police officers come to harm,' said D'Arcy but it didn't sound like he meant it. 'However, it has nothing to do with Mr Forrester.'

'I assume he can account for his whereabouts between four and eleven?'

'I were in the Nag's Head,' said Forrester. 'Getting bladdered.'

'I think we can all believe that,' said D'Arcy, acutely conscious of the strong smell of alcohol in the room.

'Does the name Alex Mather mean anything to you?' asked Blizzard.

Forrester shook his head. 'Never heard of him,' he said.

Before Blizzard could reply, there was a knock on the door and Arthur Ronald walked in.

'A word, please, John,' he said, gesturing for the inspector to follow him into the corridor.

Once out of the room, Blizzard took one look at the grim look on the superintendent's face and sighed.

'I can guess what's eating you,' said Blizzard.

'Yes, well, I hope you've got a damned good reason for lifting Nathaniel Callaghan's grandson or we'll all be checking the terms of our police pensions. I've already had a call from the chief.'

'My, my,' said Blizzard, 'doesn't news travel fast?'

* * *

Just before dawn and struggling to keep his eyes open, Blizzard guided his car through the darkness shrouding the flatlands to the west of the city, deliberately selecting a route that took him along the lane on which stood Alex Mather's cottage. Approaching the house, Blizzard saw a uniformed officer illuminated in the beam of his headlights, stamping his feet to keep warm. The inspector slowed down, leaned over and wound down the window.

'Draw the short straw then?' he said to the young constable. 'All quiet?'

'Stopped a car just before midnight. He worked for the local newspaper. A photographer. Do you want his name?'

'No, it's alright. They were making a pest of themselves all evening until we gave them something else to report on. What did you do with him?'

'Sent him on his way.'

'Good lad.'

'How's DC Mather, sir?'

'Hanging on,' said Blizzard, 'but only just.'

He wound the window back up and drove through a series of lanes until he arrived at the village where he lived. Having parked on the driveway of his modern detached home and keeping as quiet as possible, the inspector unlocked the front door and walked into the darkened hallway. He stood and listened hard but heard nothing, then caught the sound of the first sob. The landing light went on and he looked up to see Fee standing at the top of the stairs with the squirming baby in her arms.

'Your turn,' she said.

Blizzard sighed.

'Give me crooks any day,' he said.

Chapter ten

'You look like shite, John,' said Ronald when the detectives met up in the superintendent's office shortly after 8am.

'Nothing like a supportive senior officer,' said Blizzard wearily. He reached for his mug of tea. 'And you're nothing like – I'll leave you to finish the punchline, I'm too tired.'

'Baby Michael not helping, I take it?'

'Little bugger hardly slept. Fee's at the end of her tether. Thank God for Thomas the Tank Engine, I say.' The inspector held up his mug. 'You got any sugar?'

'You don't take sugar.'

'I do today.'

'Well, I don't have any, not since the doctor told me to lose weight.' Ronald flicked through the sheaf of papers on his desk and gave his friend a rueful look. 'He also told me to reduce my stress levels. Some hope with you around. I've already had two more calls from the chief about Nathaniel Callaghan. Organised Crime and Special Branch have been bending his ear about him. You know the Callaghans are off-limits, John.'

'I know but it was an accident, Arthur. We had no idea that the kid would be there. And for once, I've played it by the book. The moment I realised who he was I kicked him out. Despite protests from Chris Ramsey, I might add.'

'About what?'

'Come on, Arthur, you know the answer. We have built our success on the principle that no one is untouchable but the first time we get a crack at the Callaghans, we let it slip through our fingers. Nathaniel's lawyer complained, I take it?'

'Thankfully not, but you make sure you stay away from the Callaghans, John. Mind, their lawyer is just about the only one who hasn't complained.' Ronald held up a stack of email print-outs. 'Do you know how many protests we have had after last night?'

'The end justifies the means, Arthur.'

Blizzard picked up the local morning newspaper from the desk. *Police hit back as undercover cop fights for life*, screamed the headline. He dropped the paper back onto the table.

'Tells the public we're doing something,' he said. 'And that's important with a lunatic running round shooting police officers. It would have been even worse if we had sat on our hands. Away from the politics, we should remember the punters. People will be scared stiff.'

'Yes, I know but…'

'Besides, we've charged three people with drugs offences, two with armed robbery and a couple with possession of illegal firearms already,' said Blizzard. 'Oh, and David reckons we can link videos we found at one of the flats to that armed warehouse job last month. I call that a success.'

'Point made, but we still found nothing to link any of them to the shootings, did we? We're being accused of a fishing expedition.'

'Guilty as charged, me'lud,' said Blizzard cheerfully.

'Be nice if we could tell the chief that we got somewhere on it, though. What about him?' Ronald held up one of the documents on his desk so that Blizzard could see the photograph. 'George Killick's son? Surely, he's got plenty of motive to try to kill Alex? And, according to Max, he was letting his mouth run.'

'Except his story checks out. Barrie Killick was stuck on the motorway when Alex was shot and his wife confirmed he was at home when the gunman took a pop at Mel.'

'But he could have paid someone to do it?'

'Wouldn't have said it was his style. Besides, not sure he would have enough time to get it all fixed after his father died. No, I'm more interested in his father's death, to be honest. There's something not quite right there. I told Max we could investigate it together.'

'I know you did,' said Ronald. He sighed. 'Not content with hacking off the chief, the Callaghans and every lawyer this side of the Haft, you decided to piss off Max Randall's boss as well. The words china, shop and bull spring to mind, John. It would really help me if you could tell me these things before you go making promises.'

'Max's governor been bleating, I take it? Typical of the man. If you ask me…'

'Well, who can blame him?' snapped Ronald, his attempts at controlling his irritation finally failing. 'You have undermined his authority by going to Max and…'

'Phil Glover does not have any authority.'

'Whatever you think of him, you can't escape the fact that George Killick died in Hafton Prison! And, the last time I looked, the prison is on the east side.' Ronald noticed Blizzard's disgruntled expression. 'Oh, don't look like that. I'm prepared to let you investigate Killick's death if you think there's a connection but only if Phil is kept in the loop. Is that too much to ask?'

Blizzard gave a mock salute. 'Scout's honour.'

'As I recall, you were not in the Scouts.'

'Got kicked out after three weeks. They said I was a disruptive influence.'

'There's a pattern emerging here,' murmured Ronald. His eyes alighted on another piece of paper on the desk. 'And what about Eddie Gayle? I hear you left his front door hanging by one hinge. You do remember that the chief told us to be careful with Eddie, I take it?'

'One untouchable is enough. Eddie's fair game until he turns up and gives us a rational explanation for having Alex's phone number,' said Blizzard.

'I've got the number for the local Chinese takeaway, doesn't mean I would shoot the head chef, although sometimes I am sorely tempted given what the man does to sweet and sour chicken.'

'Yes, but the head chef is not a former undercover officer whose phone number is supposed to be a closely guarded secret, is he? And Eddie did have it away on his toes. That's suspicious behaviour in my book.'

There was a knock on the door and a uniformed officer walked in.

'Sorry to interrupt,' he said, giving Blizzard a sly smile, 'but your best mate's at reception. Wants a little chat about civil liberties. He and his wife came back from her mother's eightieth to find their front door smashed in, apparently.'

'Whoops,' said Blizzard, shooting Ronald a rueful look. 'So much for on the run.'

'I knew I shouldn't have let you add him to the list,' said Ronald. 'Not after last time.'

'Yeah, well be warned,' said the uniformed officer. 'It's a long time since I've seen Eddie this steamed up.'

Steamed up indeed. Five minutes later, Blizzard and Colley were sitting in one of the interview rooms, staring across the table at a baleful Eddie Gayle. Fat, short and perspiring in his ill-fitting black suit, Gayle always reminded Colley of a little round pig. One that stank, thought the sergeant; the air in the hot little room was filled with a pungent stench and the armpits of Gayle's shirt were stained with sweat.

Next to Gayle sat Paul D'Arcy, the lawyer cool and calm – as big a contrast to his client as could be imagined. D'Arcy gave the inspector a stern look.

'This in twice in just a few hours that I am forced to highlight your errors of judgement in relation to my clients, Chief Inspector,' said the solicitor icily. 'First, you have to release Mr Forrester after arresting him without a shred of evidence, and now this. You had better have a good excuse for breaking into my client's house because, if not, I will have your badge, of that you can be sure.'

'Yeah,' leered Gayle, 'you'll pay for this!'

'I might stretch to paying for a new front door,' said Blizzard, 'but that's all. As for having a good excuse, your client's name came up during enquiries into the shooting of Detective Constable Alex Mather so our interest is entirely legitimate.'

'An incident that occurred when Mr Gayle was out of town, as you are well aware.'

'Can anyone prove that?'

'Half the Darby and Joan Club in Goole,' said the lawyer. 'My client arrived at half past four for his elderly mother's birthday party and he and his wife did not leave the hotel until first thing this morning. I am sure Reception will confirm it.'

'Yeah,' said Gayle, jabbing a finger at Blizzard. 'Harassment, that's what this is, and you was warned last time. We'll be making an official complaint about this.'

'Yes, I'm sure you will,' said Blizzard calmly. 'But for the moment, I am more interested in finding out if there is a connection between you and Alex Mather.'

'I don't make a habit of socialising with coppers.' Gayle shot the detectives a mocking smile that revealed crooked teeth. 'Don't like the smell.'

He sat back in his chair to reveal a stomach bursting through his shirt and looked pleased with his quip.

'You never did have much of a sense of self-awareness, did you, Eddie?' said Colley, still struggling to cope with the stench in the room.

'Eh?'

'You might not like socialising with us,' said Blizzard, 'but presumably you don't mind a nice natter on the phone?'

The inspector held up an evidence bag containing the page from the notebook.

'Care to explain this?' he asked.

For the first time in the interview, Eddie Gayle looked worried.

'Careless, Eddie,' said Blizzard. 'Very careless. Not like you to make a mistake like that.'

'You had no right to…'

'I had every right,' rasped Blizzard. He leaned across the table until their faces were only a couple of feet apart and he was assailed by Gayle's foul breath. 'I have a detective fighting for his life and another officer who could have been killed if the gunman had learned to shoot straight. If I find out you were involved in any way…'

Blizzard did not finish the sentence but sat back and left it hanging in the air.

'Would someone please explain what is going on?' asked the lawyer. He gestured to the evidence bag which Blizzard had placed on the desk in front of him. 'What precisely is that?'

'That,' said Blizzard, 'is Alex Mather's mobile number, which was discovered in a drawer in your client's house.'

'A locked drawer,' said Gayle.

'Locked or not, a police officer's phone number does not prove anything,' said the lawyer.

'Doesn't it?' said Blizzard. 'I think you rang Alex, Eddie, I think you were checking if he was home. I take it you won't mind us looking at your phone?'

'I ain't saying nothing,' said Gayle in a surly voice. 'I didn't make no phone call and I know nowt about this Mather bloke.'

'Come now, Eddie,' said Blizzard. 'Don't tell me you don't know that he provided information for the Vice Squad for years, including into some of your more nefarious activities? And the fact that you were whooping it up with a bunch of old ladies in the fleshpots of Goole doesn't mean that you didn't hire someone to kill him.'

'That is the most preposterous thing I have ever heard,' said the lawyer. 'If you have evidence that my client is involved in the shooting of Detective Constable Mather then I suggest you tell us. Otherwise this interview is at an end.'

'Police officers jealously guard their privacy,' said Blizzard. 'And the fact that Eddie had…'

'Pure speculation,' snorted the lawyer, standing up. 'Last night was a fishing exercise, Chief Inspector. Something to make you look good because of your poor crime statistics. A PR stunt. Come on Eddie, we're going.'

'Can we see your mobile before you go?' asked Blizzard.

'I lost it.'

'Funny that,' said Blizzard.

'Come on, Eddie,' said D'Arcy. 'We're going.'

'Just don't leave town,' said Blizzard. He waited for them to reach the door before adding, 'Oh, lay off the Darby and Joan, Eddie. Could get you into all kinds of bother!'

Having ushered the two men out of the station, Colley returned to the interview room where a weary Blizzard was sitting with his eyes closed.

'What actually is Darby and Joan?' asked the sergeant.

'Fuck knows,' said Blizzard, not opening his eyes. 'Anyway, go away, I'm asleep.'

'So, what do you think?' asked the sergeant, ignoring the comment and grimacing as he sat down on the other side of the table. 'Eugh, Eddie was sitting on this one and it's damp.'

'He is certainly a loathsome man,' said the inspector, with his eyes still closed. 'As to what I think, I think I hate colic.'

'It would explain why Eddie was so irritable.'

Blizzard smiled and finally opened his eyes.

'I think that Eddie is hiding something from us,' he said.

'He usually is. Do you want to get a warrant, search his house again?'

'No. You can bet your bottom dollar that if he did make the call, he's long since thrown the phone in the river.'

There was a knock on the door and a uniformed officer walked in.

'Message for you,' he said, handing over a piece of paper.

Blizzard's eyes widened as he read it.

'This a wind-up?' he asked.

'Apparently not. Yer man wants to meet.'

Blizzard stood up and unhooked his jacket from the back of the chair and looked at Colley.

'Seems that we may be in line for an audience with criminal royalty,' he said.

* * *

Five minutes later, Blizzard was sitting in Arthur Ronald's office, enjoying the amazed expression on the superintendent's face.

'Nathaniel Callaghan wants to see *you?'* said Ronald.

'Yeah, apparently he has long admired my contribution to community policing and wanted to express his appreciation in person.'

'Oh, ha ha,' said Ronald. 'He does know that we let his grandson go I take it?'

'He does, yes. Seems that's not the end of it, though.'

‘I’ll have to run this past the chief first.’ Ronald picked up the desk phone and dialled an internal number. ‘Hi, Mary, it’s Arthur Ronald, is he in? Yes, it’s important.’

Chapter eleven

I was as surprised as anyone when the call came. Everyone knows about Nathaniel Callaghan and I appreciate that it put you in a difficult position, that it made you look like your authority was being undermined by me. However, when someone like Nathaniel Callaghan insists on seeing you, you can hardly say no, can you? I have to admit, though, that the thought of renewing my acquaintance with him made me uneasy and not many villains do that.

Two hours later, Blizzard and Colley were sitting in the inspector's car, which was parked outside a non-descript two-storey office block on the edge of Leeds and being filmed by a raft of CCTV cameras.

'I'm amazed we're being allowed to do this,' said Colley with a shake of the head. 'I mean, look at the place, guv, it's like Fort Knox. No one gets to see Nathaniel Callaghan. No one. Certainly not the likes of us.'

'And we nearly didn't.'

'So, what changed?'

'When I told Nathaniel's people that the chief had blocked their request for a meeting, the man himself rang up headquarters playing merry hell. If I was unpopular with the chief before, it's ten times worse now. Making him reverse a decision, particularly on my behalf, is hardly good for his reputation. Or mine.'

'It'll go down well with the troops, though. They have no time for all this untouchable malarkey. Chris Ramsey will be chuffed when he hears – he's been wittering on about how we let the kid go.'

'Yes, well let's keep it quiet for the moment, eh? We don't know what he wants to say to us yet. And if we are going after Callaghan, the last thing we want is for it to be the talk of the station.'

'But you're clearly thinking that going after him may be a possibility?' asked Colley, eying him keenly.

Blizzard grinned. 'Oh, yeah,' he said.

'Good man. Have you met Nathaniel Callaghan before? I heard he started out in Hafton.'

'A couple of times when he was a low-level thief over on the east side years ago. I was just a rookie but I seem to recall we caught him and his brother with a truck full of fruit that they'd nicked from a warehouse down on the docks.'

'What's he like?'

'You'll find him a most charming man.'

'Charming?' said Colley. 'Not sure that's the word I'd use, from what I hear. The man's as cold blooded as they come, isn't he?'

'You'll see.'

'Are the stories not true then?'

'Yeah, they're true,' said Blizzard. 'They're a different league these days, the Callaghans.'

'How come? It's a far cry from a few boxes of bruised fruit on Hafton docks.'

'It started when they supplied firearms to the IRA in the Eighties and they never looked back. Word is that half the extremists in Europe get their weapons from the Callaghans now. Everyone from Chechens to Islamic State.'

'But none of the Callaghans have been done for any of it?'

'Nathaniel and his sons don't get their hands dirty unless they really have to, which is why the request for this meeting is so intriguing.'

'That's one word for it.' Colley looked up at the cameras focused on the inspector's car. 'I heard that the Regional Organised Crime Unit have been after them for years.'

'Everyone's been after them for years, David. Special Branch, Anti-Terrorist, Interpol, the lot, but nobody can get any of it to stick. There's always been rumours that they are protected by some influential people.'

'Cops?'

'Maybe.'

'I assume we're here because of his grandson?' asked the sergeant, looking across to the building again. 'I heard that Nathaniel hates drugs.'

'Yeah, he's a strange mix. A big religious man, church on a Sunday, insisted his kids went to Sunday School, regards drugs as evil yet he is happy to ship off crates of guns to any passing loony who fancies shooting innocent civilians. Work that one out.'

'No one told him that it's double-standards?'

'No one tells Nathaniel Callaghan anything,' said Blizzard, noticing movement through one of the ground floor windows. 'Don't be fooled by the religious stuff, though. Like you say, he's ruthless. Word is there's two or three who crossed him and ended up in the Haft and I don't mean for baptism. And rumour says that he once killed a man by driving a power drill through his eye.'

'So, he's perfectly capable of setting up a hit on Alex?' For the first time in the conversation, the sergeant's voice exhibited signs of nerves. 'Or any of us?'

'Relax, David. If Nathaniel Callaghan had set it up, there's no way his man would have missed. If you ask me… ah, we're on.'

A shaven-headed man in a dark suit emerged from the building and walked towards the car. He beckoned for them to follow him and a couple of minutes later, having been searched by another of Callaghan's men, they were sitting at a mahogany desk in a first-floor office. Sitting on the other side of the desk and eying them with his piercing blue eyes was a thin man who had wispy white hair, a goatee beard and who was dressed in an expensive grey suit. Colley tried to look at ease but was acutely conscious that his palms were moist. Blizzard, for his part, seemed to be enjoying the experience.

'So, you're the man who had my grandson arrested,' said Callaghan.

'That's me,' said Blizzard. 'I take it that's why you wanted to see us?'

'Actually, I don't normally make a habit of meeting police officers.'

Blizzard noticed that music was playing low in the background. He strained to make it out and Callaghan smiled.

'Verdi,' he said. 'Do you like classical music, Chief Inspector?'

'Er, not really. More of a Coldplay man.'

'Ah. Pity.'

A young woman brought in a tray containing a china teapot and milk jug with three cups and saucers. Callaghan waited until she had poured the drinks.

'Thank you, Jane,' he said as she left the room. 'Help yourselves to biscuits, gentlemen. The ones in the gold wrappers are very pleasant, got them shipped over from Belgium.'

Callaghan studied the inspector more closely as the detective took a sip of tea.

'I fancy we have met?' he said.

'Many years ago,' said Blizzard, reaching for a biscuit. 'I was working CID on Hafton's east side. You'd been half-inching fruit from one of the warehouses down on the river. You got stopped because the lorry didn't have a tax disc. Not the kind of mistake you'd make now, I fancy.'

Colley looked nervous at the comment, glancing at Callaghan and seeking signs of irritation at the inspector's impertinence. Callaghan's mouth smiled but his eyes did not.

'Ah, yes,' said Callaghan. 'I never forget a police officer's face.'

The meaning was not lost on the officers and Colley felt his throat go dry. He unwrapped a biscuit to make himself feel better. Blizzard, for his part, looked calmly across the desk.

'I take it you want to talk about Luke?' said the inspector. 'If so, you'll know that I released him the moment I realised he was your grandson.'

'Bailed not released, Chief Inspector.' There was an edge to Callaghan's voice. 'There's a difference, as I am sure you can appreciate.'

'Not sure I had any alternative, Nathaniel. He did have a considerable amount of cannabis in his possession. I can't ignore that.'

'My grandson can be a very foolish young man, Chief Inspector. As you know, I have always counselled against the use of drugs but young Luke…' Callaghan sighed. 'I rather hoped you might regard this as a youthful indiscretion.'

'Some indiscretion, Nathaniel. There was more than just for personal use. The boy had six hundred quid on him. I think your grandson has been dealing.'

'Yes, but cannabis, Chief Inspector?' Callaghan looked at him closely. 'Are you really going to get heavy over a bit of weed? Many forces regard it as a somewhat minor offence these days. Indeed, there are some chief constables who would like to see it legalised.'

'Call us old-fashioned but we don't see it the same way.' It was Blizzard's turn to look at him closely. 'Tell me, Nathaniel, why are we here? Surely you could click your fingers and make this go away? I'm sure you have some very influential friends. You don't need me to get your grandson off the hook.'

'True enough, Chief Inspector, but I confess I had an ulterior motive for wanting to see you. I understand you were looking for the man who shot your detective when you arrested Luke?'

'Yeah, we were. We did not even know that Luke was at the house when we raided it – we certainly weren't looking for him.'

'And you did not find the gunman?'

'No, not yet.'

'What if we could help each other, Chief Inspector? What if you agreed not to prosecute my grandson and I offered you something that might help you in your enquiries, in return?'

'What did you have in mind?' asked Blizzard.

'I could ask around a few of my associates, see if I could turn up a name for you.'

'And why would you do that?'

'My grandson is different to the other men in the family, Chief Inspector.' Callaghan sighed again. 'He is more, how shall we say it? Artistic. Naïve. I do not think that he would cope well with prison, if it were it to come to that.'

'Like anyone would dare harm Nathaniel Callaghan's grandson,' said Blizzard. 'No, I think it's more likely that people like you get twitchy when someone targets a police officer because it means we pull out all the stops to catch them. If you give up the shooter, we go back to our pipe and slippers.'

Colley looked nervously at Callaghan.

'You police officers are so suspicious,' said Callaghan with a cold smile. He stood up. 'Anyway, my offer is a serious one, Chief Inspector. Do we have a deal?'

'I'd have to check with my boss.'

'I appreciate that.' Callaghan gestured to the door where the shaven-headed man had reappeared. 'Do let me know when you have an answer. Neil will see you out.'

* * *

Five minutes later the officers were walking back to the inspector's vehicle.

'Jesus!' exclaimed Colley when he judged they were far enough away from the building. 'Talk about an unholy alliance! You and Nathaniel Callaghan. Is he serious about wanting to help?'

'Doubt it.'

'He certainly seemed pissed off when you suggested his offer was not genuine. Did you see the look on his face?'

'Doesn't take much to make the Prince Charming act go away, does it? Chris is right, I should have stood up for what I believed in.' Blizzard let them into the vehicle and started the engine. 'Come on, I think it's time we tried to make sense of all this. Time for a walk on the sleazy side of life, I think.'

* * *

Nathaniel Callaghan stood at the window of his office and watched thoughtfully as the vehicle disappeared. When it had gone, he walked over to the desk and reached into a drawer, from which he removed a small red address book. He flicked through the pages until he reached the one he wanted, picked up the desk phone and dialled a number.

'Eddie,' he said. 'Nathaniel Callaghan. Tell me everything you know about John Blizzard.'

Chapter twelve

It was just after 2.30pm when Arthur Ronald's office door swung open. The superintendent looked wearily up from his paperwork and his eyes widened with surprise as he saw the chief constable.

'Sir,' said Ronald, standing up.

'Arthur,' said the chief, gesturing for him to sit back down.

'You didn't need to come over here, sir. I'd have come over to…'

'I needed the exercise.' The chief patted his paunch, sat down at the desk, looked round the office and noticed the gaffer tape holding one of the water pipes in place. 'Haven't been here for ages, you forget how crappy Abbey Road is. I'll have to ask the finance girl to see if we can't get it replaced.'

'Heard that one before.'

The chief gave a rueful smile. 'I am sure you have, Arthur. Now, to business, this deal with Nathaniel Callaghan. There's no way I can sanction anything like that. This force does not do deals with criminals. Never has, never will, as long as I'm in the job. I can't let Callaghan's grandson go scot-free when I've been on breakfast television spouting forth about the dangers of cannabis.'

'I agree, sir, so will Blizzard. I know he's already regretting the decision to bail him. I take it you do realise that if we charge the boy, there's no way Callaghan will give us the name of the man who shot Alex?'

'He might. If he's involved in something in Hafton, he'll not want Blizzard stampeding all over the place in his inimitable manner, kicking down doors. Callaghan is a ruthless man, he would think nothing about screwing someone over if it meant protecting his organisation.'

'So, are you saying we can investigate him?' asked Ronald, not sure he was hearing right.

'Officially, no.'

'And unofficially?'

'Who knows what this inquiry may turn up, Arthur.'

'Can I ask why the change of mind, sir? I mean, won't Special Branch object?'

'Already have. I've just come off the phone from a bright-eyed kid fresh out of university – Sebastian Twiston-Frecklington or something – telling me what I can and can't do. They want charges dropped against Luke Callaghan because charging him would compromise their ongoing investigations.'

'What ongoing investigations?'

'Exactly. Look, Arthur, I can't sanction any of this officially but I'll do what I can to watch your back.'

'And if things go wrong?'

'Same deal as with Keeper.' The chief stood up. 'I knew nothing about that officially, remember. Oh, and remind Blizzard to lay off Eddie Gayle, will you? I've just had an official complaint from his lawyer. Something about a new door. If we are going after the Callaghans, I don't want Gayle getting in the way. Nice and quietly does it. I take it Blizzard does know what nice and quietly means?'

He strode down the corridor, leaving Ronald deep in thought.

Eventually, the superintendent dialled Blizzard's number. Blizzard and Colley were back in Hafton, in a rundown street on the edge of the city centre when the inspector's mobile rang. Blizzard took the call as they walked towards a dilapidated snooker club on the corner.

'It's Arthur,' said a voice. He sounded serious. 'You alone?'

'Just me and David.'

'Well I want you to keep this between the two of you. I've got word back from the chief.'

'That was quick. Doesn't take long to say no, I guess.'

'He won't do a deal on the grandson, granted, but he doesn't mind if you keep looking into Callaghan's affairs.'

'Officially?' said Blizzard as the officers approached the snooker hall.

'I said it was complicated.'

The line went dead. Blizzard looked at Colley.

'I have this awful feeling that we're being set up,' he said. 'We can go after Callaghan.'

'Marvellous,' sighed Colley. 'I never wanted to see my daughter grow up anyway.'

This time, Blizzard did not try to reassure him and the two officers walked from the brightness of the street into the darkness of the dingy snooker hall.

'You do know how to show a boy a good time,' said Colley, his nostrils wrinkling at the musty, damp smell.

'Yeah, sorry about that but this is where the slimeballs hang out.'

'Get away.'

Once their eyes had grown accustomed to the murk, they saw that play had stopped on the three occupied tables and that the players were looking at them suspiciously, cues in hand.

'Nice to be welcomed,' said Colley. He noticed a small man in a scruffy brown overcoat skulking along the far wall and glancing furtively at the detectives as he headed for the nearest door. 'That your man?'

'That's him, yes. Sammy B. But first, to make this look good... I don't want them thinking we're looking for him.'

Blizzard walked up to one of the tables.

'I'm looking for a man in a leather jacket,' he said loudly, holding up his warrant card. 'He is wanted in connection with a street robbery. A witness saw him run in here. Anyone see him?'

The players shook their heads.

'And would you tell me if you had?' asked Blizzard.

'No fucking chance,' said a voice in the darkness, but the detectives could not see who had spoken.

Blizzard walked up to the nearest player, a shaven-headed man wearing a black T-shirt and tatty jeans. The man's knuckles glowed white as he gripped his cue.

'What about you,' said Blizzard. 'You seen him?'

'Na.'

Blizzard fixed him with steely blue eyes.

'If I find that he has been in here and you knew about it...' He did not finish the sentence. The man turned away.

The detectives left the hall, emerging with relief into the fresh air of the street, where they saw the man in the long coat scuttling away. They caught up with him at the corner, Blizzard grasping him by the arm. The man, a weasel-faced character with lank black hair and bad skin, winced.

'You're hurting me,' he squealed.

'Oh, dear, what a pity,' said Blizzard. 'Not running away from us, were you?'

'If anyone sees me talking to you, I'm dead meat.'

'I'll tell the lot of them you're my informant if I don't get some answers,' said the inspector. 'I'm sick of people playing games.'

'You wouldn't do that, Mister Blizzard.'

'Try me.' Blizzard glanced along the street. 'I reckon some of your mates will be leaving the club in the next few minutes now they know we're around so unless you want them to see our cosy little tête-à-tête, talk to me and talk fast.'

'What do you want to know?' asked Sammy B anxiously.

'Someone tried to kill two police officers last night and I think you knew it was going to happen.'

'I don't know nothing about that, Mister Blizzard. Honest. I'd have told you if I did.'

'Try again, Sammy. You were spooked the last time I saw you and you're spooked now. I think it's because you knew that someone was going to shoot Alex Mather.'

'You've got it all wrong.'

'Then enlighten me.'

'I can't.'

'Listen,' said the inspector, squeezing Sammy B's arm tighter so that his informant squirmed. 'I've had virtually no sleep so don't fuck me around. You know who did it, don't you?'

'I don't know nothing about no hit on your officer. Honest, Mister Blizzard. I were as surprised as anyone when it happened. Everyone was. Whoever did it, he ain't from one of the gangs.'

'But you did know something was going to happen?'

Sammy hesitated. 'Maybe,' he said eventually, lowering his voice. 'But this must never come from me, these people are dangerous.'

'So am I.'

'No offence, Mister Blizzard, but you ain't got nothing on them. You seen what happened to George Killick.'

'What's he got to do with this?'

'That were the word,' blurted out Sammy B. He glanced fearfully along the deserted street towards the snooker hall. 'That was what was spooking everyone. We all knew that Killick was going to be topped in prison. Someone had put out a contract to have it done.'

'Why didn't you tell me?' exclaimed Blizzard.

'No one cares if a kiddy fiddler gets topped, Mister Blizzard. Whoever did it did society a favour, I reckon.'

'If you can't tell us who did it, can you tell us how much?' asked Colley.

'I heard ten grand.'

Colley gave a low whistle.

'What did George Killick know that was worth ten grand to shut him up?' asked Blizzard.

'It's more than my life's worth to tell you that, Mr Blizzard.' Sammy B gave him a pathetic look. 'It might not be a great life but it's all I've got.'

Two men emerged from the snooker hall and looked in their direction.

'If I tell you, can I go?' asked Sammy B quickly.

Blizzard nodded.

'You missed one,' said Sammy B. 'When you put them kiddy fiddlers away, you missed one. The one that organised it all. That's why folks is panicking. Even hard men get frightened when…' He slapped a hand over his mouth.

Blizzard glanced at the sergeant; they were both thinking the same thing.

'Are we talking about Nathaniel Callaghan, by any chance?' asked Blizzard in a low voice. 'Is he the one behind the contract?'

'Keep your voice down,' hissed Sammy B, fear etched into his face. 'I ain't never going to talk about him. What I do know is that Killick was murdered because he was trying to do a deal.'

'What kind of deal?'

'With one of your lot,' said Sammy B. 'He was going to give up the main man in return for getting out with a new identity. I heard Killick had tried to slash his wrists twice. Couldn't take it no more.'

'Who was he talking to?' asked Blizzard. 'Who's the copper?'

'Some bloke on the east side. Glover, I think he's called.'

'Phil Glover? The DCI? You sure?'

Sammy B nodded.

'And whoever it was found out what they were planning to do?' asked Colley.

'Killick's dead, ain't he?' said Sammy B, giving a leer that revealed crooked and nicotine-stained teeth. 'You work it out.'

He squirmed free of the inspector's grasp and scuttled off down the street. The detectives did not try to stop him.

'Nathaniel Callaghan a paedophile?' asked Colley. 'I mean, God fearing, Bible-bashing Nathaniel into kids?'

'Takes all sorts,' said Blizzard. 'Think back to when we lifted the rest. You wouldn't have put any of them down as child abusers, would you? Rotary's finest. That's how they get away with it, hiding in plain sight.'

'I guess.'

'And what about Phil Glover?' said Blizzard with a shake of the head. 'What on earth is he playing at?'

'Glory boy?' said Colley. 'You did get a lot of headlines when the sex ring guys were locked up. Now suddenly he gets presented with the chance to put away the main man and make you look stupid at the same time.'

'Or perhaps we've got it all wrong,' murmured Blizzard as they started to walk back towards the inspector's car. 'What if he was trying to protect the main man instead? Perhaps he was trying to find out what Killick knew, what he was prepared to tell. Perhaps that's why he does not want Max investigating Killick's death.'

'Oh, come off it, guv.'

'Look, when we were running Keeper, we always suspected that the chief was the one protecting them from getting nicked but…'

'You were the only one who believed that,' said Colley. 'One of your conspiracy theories. Besides, are you really telling me that Phil Glover is bent? Never. Straight as they come, that one.'

'You sure?' Blizzard shot him a look. 'I mean, can you say, hand on heart, that you know the man that well that you can swear Phil Glover is clean? Would you swear it on Laura's life?'

They walked in silence for a few moments.

'Permission to swear,' said Colley as they reached the car.

'Granted.'

'Bugger, bollocks and bastards.'

'Very eloquently put, Sergeant,' said Blizzard. 'Perhaps you should become an inspector, after all.'

* * *

Ronnie Forrester was sitting at his usual corner table in the pub shortly after 6pm, working his way through his third pint, when Eddie Gayle walked into the bar.

'They let you out then?' said Forrester as Gayle walked over to his table.

'Typical Blizzard,' said Gayle. He sat down and reached over to take a swig of Forrester's ale. 'A load of hot air. D'Arcy shut him up, like he always does. But Blizzard knows something, I'm sure of it.'

'Like what?' Forrester looked worried. 'What does he know?'

'He's been given permission to investigate George Killick's death.'

'I thought Phil Glover had put a stop to that?'

'Yeah, well you heard wrong.' Gayle scowled. 'Max Randall went running to Blizzard. And that means trouble, Ronnie. You know what Blizzard's like when he gets his teeth into something.'

'Only too well.'

'What's more,' said Gayle. 'Nathaniel is panicking. Wants to make sure no one follows George Killick's example.'

'So, what do we do?'

'I think it's time for another prison visit. Remind our Mister Roberts that he needs to keep his mouth shut when Blizzard comes knocking.'

'There's another way of dealing with it,' said Forrester quietly. He glanced around to make sure that no one was listening. 'I'm going to have Blizzard killed.'

Gayle stared at him in astonishment.

'Surely you're not serious?' he said. 'Hitting Mather was stupid enough but Blizzard? You're mad.'

'If Mather knows about the guns, then so does Blizzard.'

'Yes, and half the bloody police force. Killing a couple of them won't make a difference.'

'That does not matter. Once people find out I was the one who ordered the shootings, no one will dare talk to the police. This is about sending out a message, Eddie. Besides, I'll be doing us all a favour getting rid of Blizzard. He's had it coming for years.'

'Granted but what happens when Nathaniel finds out what you're doing?' asked Gayle. 'Blizzard will be the least of your worries then.'

'In a day or two, Nathaniel Callaghan will be history,' said Forrester, taking a swig of beer. 'There's a new top man now.'

'Your funeral,' said Gayle, standing up. 'And you just keep me out of it.'

Chapter thirteen

Did I think that Phil Glover was bent after talking to Sammy B? Can you blame me if I did? I mean, our big dread with Keeper had always been that someone high up in the force was protecting the members of the sex ring and now here we were being told that Phil had been spending time with George Killick without telling anyone on the inquiry. Yes, I know, pot calling the kettle black but we kept Keeper secret because no one believed us and we did not know who we could trust. I mean, what the hell was I supposed to think? Was Callaghan the one putting the money up to kill Killick? Was that his dark little secret? Was that why Max was being warned off?

And what was I to think about you granting me permission to investigate Callaghan when everyone else usually gets told to steer clear? Ever since Keeper, I've been increasingly paranoid, I know that, probably got it from Alex Mather, but I couldn't help thinking that if I went against Callaghan and it blew up in my face you would be able to fire me, no questions asked. Rogue copper ignoring the rules one time too many. It would allow you to get rid of a thorn in your side.

Detective Chief Inspector Phil Glover, a thin, bespectacled and balding man, sat in furious silence as he stared across his desk and listened to Blizzard shortly before noon the following morning. Sitting next to Blizzard was an uncomfortable Max Randall, watching in alarm as his boss's thunderous expression darkened with every word that his friend uttered. Finally, Blizzard fell silent.

'Finished?' said Glover through pursed lips. 'Nothing else to add?'

Blizzard shook his head. 'I think I've said enough.'

'Too fucking right you have!' Glover's tone was cold and clipped. 'How dare you come into my office and suggest that I'm involved in the death of George Killick? I know you've not got much time for me, John, but even by your standards this is an outrage.'

'How else am I supposed to interpret it?' protested Blizzard. 'George Killick dies and, lo and behold, we find out that you have been talking to him and trying to stop Max asking awkward questions about his death. Add two and two and it usually comes to four.'

'Or five. I take it you put him up to this, Max?' Glover gave Randall a hard look. 'Your governor doesn't back you up, so you go running to your old mate? That the way of it?'

'It wasn't like that,' said Randall defensively. 'The shooting of Alex Mather changed everything. However, it does make me wonder. I mean, why didn't you tell me what was happening with Killick right from the off? Don't you trust me?'

'I don't trust *him*,' said Glover, nodding towards Blizzard. 'The last thing I wanted was him blundering in and fucking things up for me.'

'That's it, isn't it?' sneered Blizzard. 'You just couldn't stand me getting all the headlines the last time so you keep everything to yourself this time around. You're a glory boy, Phil.'

'That's ironic coming from you!'

'Better than the alternative.' Blizzard was going to continue when something stopped him.

'Go on,' said Glover, 'get it said. What's the alternative?'

'That you are covering for someone. Something in your back pocket, was it?'

'I demand you take that back!' exclaimed Glover. He half stood up and angrily jabbed a finger at his colleague. 'How dare you?'

For a moment, it looked like Glover was going to strike the inspector but with an immense effort, he sat back down and gave himself a few seconds to calm down. Now, he sounded hurt.

'I may be many things but bent is not one of them,' he said.

Noticing Glover's expression and the unease on Randall's face, Blizzard realised that he'd gone too far and nodded.

'OK, I apologise,' he said, holding up his hands. 'That was out of order. Didn't get much sleep last night.'

'That's no excuse for saying something like that. We're all tired and I, for one, am tired of you ignoring the rules. We're all on the same side, you know. This isn't the John Blizzard Show although sometimes you could be forgiven for thinking it is.'

An awkward silence settled on the room as both men brooded over what had been said. Randall stared out of the window wishing he was somewhere else. He was beginning to regret involving Blizzard in the inquiry. Eventually it was Blizzard who spoke, recalling Ronald's comments earlier in the morning and trying to sound more conciliatory towards Glover.

'So,' he said, 'did you get the name of the man Killick was going to give up?'

'He was going to let me have it when I had the deal in place.' Glover's reply was clipped. Cold. Professional.

'And what exactly was the deal?' asked Blizzard.

'An extra third off his sentence so he could be moved immediately to an open prison away from Hafton and a new identity and protection when he got out. Killick was small fry compared with the ringleader so I thought it was worth it.'

'You're probably right,' said Blizzard.

'What, you're actually agreeing with me?'

'For once, yes, Phil. If Nathaniel Callaghan is behind this and we can prove that…'

'Hang on, where does Callaghan come into this?' Glover looked genuinely surprised. 'Nobody has mentioned him.'

'I am wondering if he was the name Killick was going to give you. Just a theory.'

'Yes, well, I suggest you keep your theories to yourself when it comes to him,' said Glover tartly. 'You know the chief's view – no one investigates Callaghan without official say so.'

Blizzard hesitated. Could he afford to take Phil Glover into his confidence? Was Glover passing information to Callaghan? Maybe, decided Blizzard, it was time to let the rabbit run.

'Actually,' he said, 'I was with Callaghan yesterday and…'

'You've seen him?' Glover stared at Blizzard in amazement. 'You've seen Nathaniel Callaghan?'

'We lifted his grandson during the raids. Drug dealing. Callaghan wanted us to drop the case.'

'I'll bet he does. And I bet you've been warned off by Special Branch as well.'

Blizzard looked at him suspiciously. 'And how would you know that?' he said.

'Nothing sinister,' said Glover, allowing himself a slight smile. 'Callaghan was involved in something we stumbled across when I was with Organised Crime – some guns turned up in a warehouse down by the docks and Special Branch told us to drop it.'

'And did you?'

'What do you think?'

'Let's forget Nathaniel Callaghan for the moment,' said Blizzard. 'Let's talk about George Killick. Max thinks there's something odd about his death and so do I. Maybe one of the cons put two and two together, worked out what Killick was planning to tell you and passed the word on to whoever needed to know?'

'Not sure how anyone could know. I was very discreet. Let it be known that I wanted to talk to him about a fraud from when he ran his estate agency.'

'Yeah, like they wouldn't see through that,' said Blizzard.

Glover frowned but said nothing.

'So why discourage me from investigating?' asked Randall. 'I mean, once he was dead, the deal was not going to happen.'

'I didn't want to go charging without any evidence.' Glover shot Blizzard a look. 'Causes more trouble than it's worth.'

Blizzard decided to say nothing.

'Besides,' continued Glover, 'the examination by the prison doctor suggested natural causes so I asked for a PM. I wanted to be sure.'

'Who's doing the PM?' asked Blizzard.

'Reynolds, 2pm at the General. Want to go with Max?' Glover allowed himself a slight smile. 'I know how well you and Peter Reynolds get on.'

'If you're sure I'm not standing on your toes.' Blizzard tried to continue with his conciliatory tone. 'One last thing, any idea if this is anything to do with Eddie Gayle?'

'He did visit Killick a couple of days before he died but Killick would not say why. Gayle was with one of his goons. A piece of muscle called Ronnie Forrester.'

'Swarthy guy, cauliflower ear, likes wearing gold medallions?'

'Yeah, that's him.'

'I know him,' said Blizzard, a gleam in his eyes. The inspector headed for the door. 'Thanks, Phil.'

‘Anything to help,’ said Glover but he didn’t sound like he meant it.

Blizzard left the office followed by Randall, who caught his friend up half way down the corridor.

‘You and your bloody mouth,’ he said angrily when he was sure that Glover could not hear. ‘You’ll get me fired one day.’

‘Made your governor change his mind, though, didn’t I? You got your investigation.’

‘Yes, but calling him a bent copper is not exactly what I had in mind, John.’

‘Got to ask the question, Max.’

‘He’s not bent.’

‘Sure?’

‘Sure.’

‘OK but nevertheless, we continue to trust no one,’ said Blizzard as they arrived at the door to Randall’s office. ‘Someone’s leaking information about this, otherwise how would my informant know that Glover was trying to do a deal with Killick?’

‘Fair point.’

‘You going to make me a cuppa before we head off to the hospital then?’ said Blizzard as they walked into Randall’s untidy office with its paper-strewn desk. ‘I don’t suppose you have any sugar? Or can find it?’

‘The doctor warned me off sugar,’ said Randall. He crouched down to open a cupboard and held up a bag. ‘Said it was fucking up my health so, I bought some in special.’

Phil Glover waited until the sound of the detectives’ footsteps had faded away along the corridor, picked up his desk phone and dialled an internal number.

‘Is the chief in?’ he said into the receiver. ‘Thank you, I’ll wait.’

‘Problem, Phil?’ said a voice at the other end after a few moments.

'Too right there's a problem,' said Glover. 'I've just had John Blizzard in my office, shouting his mouth off about me going to see George Killick. All but said I was bent and that I'm the reason Killick is dead.'

'He's tired.'

'Maybe he is, sir, but I'm not prepared to stand for him saying that about me.'

'Just let the game play out, Phil.'

And the line went dead.

* * *

As Blizzard settled down with his cup of tea in Randall's office, his mobile rang again. Number Unknown, said the readout.

'Must have missed out on my PPI,' sighed Blizzard. He took the call.

'It's Nathaniel Callaghan,' said the voice on the other end.

'How the hell did you get my number?' snapped Blizzard, sitting up sharply.

'That's not important. I understand you are going to charge Luke.'

'We are.'

'I rather hoped we had a deal, Chief Inspector.'

'You watch much breakfast telly, Nathaniel?'

'What?'

'Our chief is a bit of a media tart. Thinks we should come down hard on anyone dealing cannabis and doesn't mind who knows it. I take it this means that you are not going to help us find whoever shot Alex Mather.'

'That rather depends, Chief Inspector.'

'Depends on what?'

'On whether you stop asking questions about me.'

Run, rabbit, run, thought Blizzard.

Chapter fourteen

The man parked the stolen vehicle in the car park at Hafton General Hospital shortly before 2pm and glanced nervously at the people streaming past him along the path on their way to afternoon visiting in the wards. His experiences the previous night had shaken his confidence and, sitting there in the wan winter afternoon light, he started to sweat as he recalled the panic that had overwhelmed him when the officer asked him to wind the window down in Waterston Lane. He sunk lower in his seat so that no one could see him.

He had always known that he was unsuitable as a hired hitman but had not been surprised when he was approached to do the job; they knew that he was desperate, willing to do just about anything to prevent a visit from the bully boys and their sledgehammers. And with no criminal record, he knew that he would be difficult for the police to track down, at least until the job was done and he could flee Hafton and make a new life for himself.

The man had never fired a gun before, had never even held one, and after the bullet failed to kill Alex Mather he had found himself torn apart by doubt after he rushed from the cottage. Sickened and tormented by what he had done, by the indelible image of Mather's blood soaking into the carpet and the strangled gurgling sound that the detective was making, he had in the hours that followed the attack toyed with the idea of handing himself in to police, explaining that he had no option but to commit the deed, that he was being forced into it. Try and do a deal.

He had quickly discounted the idea; everyone knew how the police treated those who harmed their own and with Mather fighting for his life the man knew that he could still be looking at a murder charge. He shook his head to banish the thought and reached across to open the glove compartment. The man surveyed the gun for a moment, slammed closed the compartment and settled down to wait. Let the game play out, he thought.

* * *

Rachel Mather was standing by her brother's bed when Blizzard and Randall walked into the intensive care unit shortly before 2pm. On seeing how tired she looked, her eyes red-rimmed and bloodshot, her skin pale and blotchy, the chief inspector realised how weary he also felt. His headache had started to come on again and his bad back had begun to ache.

'Any change?' he asked, looking at the peaceful figure of his friend lying in the bed, hooked up to bleeping machines.

'A bit worse,' said Rachel.

'But at least he's still alive, that's good, isn't it?' said Randall. 'I mean, it's nearly 48 hours since he was shot. Got to count for something.'

'The doctors said not to read anything into it. He's still very ill.' She looked at Randall. 'I don't think we've met.'

'Detective Inspector Max Randall. From the east side.' The detective extended a hand, noting how clammy her skin felt when she shook it. 'I worked with your brother. Is Alex going to be alright?'

'I'm not sure. The doctors are not sounding very optimistic.' Her eyes were moist. 'They're not sure he's going to wake up.'

The detectives looked at the injured man in solemn silence for a few moments.

'I wonder if I can ask you a question, Rachel?' said Blizzard eventually. 'Run a couple of names past you?'

'If you think it will help.'

'Hopefully it will,' said Blizzard. 'The first one is a man called Eddie Gayle.'

'I am afraid that I have never heard of him.'

'How about Ronnie Forrester?'

She shook her head. 'Sorry.'

Blizzard reached into his jacket pocket and produced a photocopied sheet bearing the men's photographs.

'Perhaps this will jog your memory,' he said, holding them up so that she could see. 'Do you recognise either of them?'

She examined the faces and shook her head again.

'You're fortunate then,' said Blizzard.

'They certainly don't look very pleasant. Does Alex know them?'

'They moved in the same circles when he was undercover,' replied Blizzard.

She looked across to her brother and shook her head.

'There is so much I don't know about him,' she said quietly. 'It's a different world. Do you think they had something to do with what happened to him?'

'Honest answer, Rachel?' said Blizzard. 'I don't know what to think but he provided intelligence on a lot of criminals.'

'I am beginning to realise that. One of the nurses saw something on the television that said you had raided a lot of houses and made some arrests.'

'We did. Look, I won't beat about the bush, there's a lot of people with good reason to see your brother harmed but, at the moment, we are nowhere nearer to linking any of them with the attack.'

'So why mention these two in particular?' she asked. She nodded at the pictures in his hand. 'You must have a reason.'

'Alex provided a lot of information on Eddie Gayle,' said Blizzard. 'And he has your brother's mobile phone number but we don't know why.'

'His mobile number?' She looked surprised. 'Alex hardly gives his number out to anyone. It took me ages to get it from him. You know how paranoid he is about security.'

'Which is why we are so interested in Eddie Gayle,' said Blizzard. 'Are you sure Alex never mentioned him?'

'It took him six months to tell me that he'd decided to join the police force so what do you think?' She gave a slight smile and looked across at her brother. 'Always secrets with Alex.'

'That's what I figured,' said Blizzard gloomily. He glanced at the wall clock. 'We have to go, I am afraid. Attending a post-mortem on the next floor down.'

'Is it connected to the case?'

'Possibly,' said Blizzard. 'Possibly not. I don't suppose the name George Killick rings a bell?'

'Oh, yes, I know him alright.'

The detectives exchanged glances.

'You know George Killick?' said Randall.

'He handled the sale of our house as part of the divorce settlement. That's when I went back to the name Mather. Why do you want to know about George Killick?'

'He's also dead. Possibly murdered.'

Rachel digested the information for a few moments then shook her head.

'What a world you live in,' she said. 'George seemed such a nice man. I could not believe it when I read in the paper that he had been… with those poor children…' Her voice tailed off. 'Well, you know…'

The officers nodded and walked out of the room, leaving Rachel Mather to look down upon the silent figure of her brother, alone with his secrets in a world she could not reach. It struck her that it had always been the same.

'Sleep well, brother dear,' she murmured and reached into her handbag for her mobile phone.

* * *

Eddie Gayle and Ronnie Forrester arrived at Hafton Prison shortly before 2pm, parking their 4x4 in the car park in front of the red-brick Victorian building. Gayle stood and stared up at the barred windows and shuddered. He had never been locked up despite his many nefarious activities and the thought filled him with dread. Noticing Forrester eying him intently, Gayle grunted and they made their way through the main doors and presented themselves to the reception desk.

'We're here for visiting time,' Gayle told the officer on duty.

'To see who?' she asked.

'Mark Roberts. He's in E wing.'

The officer glanced down at his list.

'He's not to receive any visitors,' she said.

'Says who?' demanded Gayle.

'Says us,' she said. 'Mr Roberts is the subject of a police inquiry and will not be seeing anyone until it has been completed.'

'Who's the investigating officer?' asked Gayle. 'We might want to make a complaint to him about this.'

'DCI Blizzard,' she said, adding with a smile. 'He says you know him.'

Gayle turned on his heel and stalked from the building. Once he had gone, the officer picked up the desk phone.

'DCI Blizzard?' she said. 'Yes, it is. Gayle and Forrester turned up like you said. I told them, yes. Unimpressed, I would say.'

‘Anything interesting?’ asked Randall as Blizzard ended the call and slipped the mobile back into his pocket and they continued to walk along the hospital corridor.

‘That was the prison. Seems we were right. Eddie Gayle and his little pal fancied a spot of visiting.’

‘Interesting,’ said Randall. ‘There’s definitely something afoot. ‘

They reached the lifts and Blizzard punched in the floor number.

‘Any reason you did not try to find out if Rachel knows Nathaniel Callaghan?’ asked Randall as they waited.

‘How could she, Max? Like she said, it’s a different world. People like her live their lives without even the foggiest notion what goes on in their city. Probably just as well. They’d never sleep if they did.’

‘Nevertheless…’

‘The man seems to have eyes and ears everywhere and I don’t want him hearing that Rachel is being asked questions about him. He might get the wrong idea and we need to protect her. Time for a spot of discretion, I think.’

‘Discretion?’ said Randall as they got into the lift. ‘A new word for you. It’s true, isn’t it? You’re never too old to learn. I reckon it’s the baby that’s turning you into a human being.’

‘Everyone a comedian,’ said Blizzard.

As the detectives got out of the lift two floors down, Randall’s mobile phone went off. He took the call.

‘It’s Colley,’ said a voice. ‘You on your way into the PM with Reynolds?’

‘Uh-uh.’

‘Well, you’re impinging on my territory so I want every spit and fart of the governor’s encounter with him, yeah?’

‘Why?’

‘I dine out on these stories, Maxie Boy,’ said Colley. ‘Every last detail, yeah? There’s a drink in it for you.’

‘Well, in that case, young man...’

'Who was that?' asked Blizzard as the detective inspector ended the call and slipped the phone back into his pocket.

'Er, one of the lads back at the factory.'

'Not David Colley asking for a full report of the PM then?' Blizzard smiled. 'He thinks I don't know.'

'You should have been a detective,' said Randall and followed Blizzard into the sterilised surroundings of the mortuary. 'You'd be good at that.'

* * *

'Ah, they said it would be you, Blizzard,' said Home Office pathologist Peter Reynolds, not looking up from his examination of the body on the slab as the detectives entered the room. 'I have to say I was rather surprised, though. I heard you'd had your wrists slapped for hacking off that nice DCI Glover.'

Reynolds finally looked up and gave Randall a sly smile.

'Max,' he said, 'what a delight, long time, no see.'

Blizzard scowled at the pathologist's pointed bonhomie towards the east-side detective, while also wondering, as he always did, where Reynolds obtained his information about the internal machinations of the force. The thought made him more determined than ever to keep any enquiries about Nathaniel Callaghan as low key as possible.

The pathologist's comment did little to improve the inspector's mood; everyone knew that he detested Reynolds. Now, the inspector surveyed him with little enthusiasm. Blizzard had never been able to understand Peter Reynolds. A balding middle-aged little man with piggy eyes gleaming out of a chubby face, and dressed in a shabby, ill-fitting black suit, Reynolds always gave the impression that he enjoyed being around death, revelled in spending time in the company of corpses. Blizzard found the idea distasteful and, without realising he had done it, he scowled.

'So,' said Reynolds, returning his attention to the body of the wiry man in his fifties, with thinning grey hair and cheeks sunken in death, 'you want to know if the rank amateur who did the somewhat cursory initial examination on our Mister Killick missed anything?'

'Something like that,' grunted Blizzard.

'Well,' said Reynolds, reaching over to a nearby table and holding up an X-Ray to the light, 'George Killick had heart trouble, I can tell you that for starters. The result of too many Freemason's dinners, I imagine. They ever ask you to join, Blizzard?'

'No.'

'There's a surprise. You'd look good with a knotted hankie on your head. Oh, while I remember, how's that delightful baby of yours? Not yet old enough to realise his misfortune in having you as a father, I suspect? A blessing indeed.'

'Just get on with it,' growled Blizzard.

'Patience, patience, my dear inspector.'

'Chief Inspector.'

'Not for much longer if those crime figures keep dropping, from what I hear,' said Reynolds, placing the X-Ray back on the table. 'One fuck-up from the sack, that's what I was told. At a Freemasons dinner, oddly enough. By one of your esteemed colleagues. Your pal Phil Glover indeed. Last night's shenanigans go well? Not going to have to take up golf to fill those long hours of retirement?'

Blizzard looked at him balefully but resisted the temptation to hurdle the dead body and drive his fist into the pathologist's face. He knew such an action would probably end his career but he couldn't help feeling that it would be worth it. For his part, Reynolds winked at Randall, who stifled a smile and wondered if anyone would notice if he slid his notebook out of his jacket and made surreptitious notes for Colley.

‘So,’ said Blizzard, suddenly conscious of a throbbing in his temple, ‘are you saying that George Killick died from a heart attack? Natural causes? Am I wasting my time?’

‘Au contraire,’ said Reynolds, humming gently as his fingers flickered over the dead man’s face in a way that made both detectives uneasy. ‘His condition might well have dispatched him to the realm of the angels but not for some years, I fancy. No, I tend to think it much more likely that your man was smothered. With a pillow, I would imagine.’

‘Murder?’ said Blizzard.

‘Bravo, very good. No wonder they made you a chief inspector.’

As Blizzard glowered at the pathologist, Max Randall stared down at the body with a gleam in his eyes.

‘I was right all along, this is dodgy,’ he said then looked at Reynolds. ‘But why did the first examination suggest natural causes?’

‘An easy mistake for a humble prison doctor to make.’ Reynolds pointed to George Killick’s mouth. ‘If you look closely, you will see that there’s discolouration round the lips. Faint I grant you, but clear enough if you know what you’re looking for.’

‘So, when did he die?’ asked Blizzard.

‘The prison doctor’s report suggests about four hours before he was found,’ replied Reynolds, moving over to the table and referring to a printed sheet. ‘I tend to concur. At least she got something right, poor girl. That and the fact that your Mister Killick is dead. She was spot on with that.’

‘That everything?’ said Blizzard, scowling at the quip.

‘I would have said that it was entirely sufficient for your requirements, Chief Inspector.’

Blizzard left the room without replying.

‘No, don’t thank me,’ murmured Reynolds.

‘Sorry,’ said Randall to the pathologist when the DCI had gone. ‘He’s not had much sleep.’

'That's elderly fathers for you,' said Reynolds. 'They need even more sleep than their babies, I find. Besides, there is no need to apologise for John Blizzard. That's what I always tell young Colley. How come he is not here?'

'Just the way it fell.'

'Well, you be sure to report back to him,' said Reynolds returning to his examination of the body, 'I understand he holds court in the canteen about our little encounters. The line about elderly fathers might go down rather well, I would venture to suggest. One does so like to please one's public.'

'I'm sure it will,' said Randall. 'Thank you.'

Reynolds inclined his head slightly and the detective inspector left the room, breaking into a jog to catch up with Blizzard, who was striding down the corridor. Randall caught up with him at the lifts as the chief inspector pressed the button.

'He's a sanctimonious bastard,' said Blizzard as one of the lifts pinged and the door slid open.

'He's certainly an odd old stick,' said Randall as they entered the lift. 'What's the next move then?'

'Time to talk to Mark Roberts,' said Blizzard. He pressed the ground floor button and, with a few creaks, the lift began to descend. 'I want to hear from his own lips how he found Killick's body. Maybe he can also tell us what links Eddie Gayle and Nathaniel Callaghan. There's a connection in there somewhere.'

'Agreed.'

They reached the ground floor and emerged into a busy corridor, weaving their way through the mass of visitors heading for the lifts. Once out into the pale afternoon sun, the officers headed across the car park. They had just arrived at the DCI's car and Blizzard was fishing in his trouser pocket for the keys when the first shot rang out. The officers knew instinctively what it was and hurled themselves behind the vehicle.

'Where the fuck did that come from?' gasped Randall, peering over the bonnet as people began to scream and run for cover.

The shrieks gave him his answer and the detectives peered out towards a small knot of trees on the far side of the car park where a figure lay motionless next to a screaming woman who was crying for help.

'There,' cried Randall, pointing to a man in a scuffed parka and jeans and a black balaclava, who was standing a few car lengths away with his gun still pointing at the man on the floor.

Noticing them watching him, the gunman turned, slipped the weapon into his jacket pocket and ran towards a black vehicle, wrenching open the driver's door. The detectives zig-zagged across the car park, keeping low to the ground, fearful lest another shot ring out. As they did so, they heard the revving of an engine and the squeal of tyres as the vehicle sped out onto the main road, narrowly missing a mother and her pushchair and moving too fast for either officer to make out the registration number. Within seconds it had vanished from view, weaving its way in among the busy traffic.

Blizzard was the first to arrive at the victim, leaving the wheezing Randall behind him. The DCI flashed his warrant card at the screaming woman and crouched over the man, whose blue T-shirt was rapidly turning crimson with blood which had spread across the tarmac. His face was grey and his eyes had rolled into the back of his head. The inspector checked for a pulse but he knew that he would not find one. Blizzard closed his eyes for a moment, the ramifications of what he was seeing playing out in his mind. Death list.

The woman's shrill screams pierced his thoughts and the inspector looked at her.

'Are you hurt?' he asked.

She shook her head.

'Who is he?' asked the inspector, glancing down at the dead man.

'My boyfriend,' she blurted out between sobs which racked her body. 'Aidan Horan.'

'I know him,' said Randall, arriving at the scene, his breathing heavy and with sweat glistening on his brow as he looked down at the victim. 'Is he alive?'

Blizzard shook his head and the woman emitted another agonised shriek and collapsed onto the floor. The inspector straightened up.

'Call it in, Max,' he said grimly as they heard the blaring of vehicle horns tracing the vehicle's get away along nearby roads. 'It would seem that our friend is getting the hang of this.'

Chapter fifteen

I don't believe in coincidences. I never have. You know that. Everyone knows about Blizzard's First Law so, to me, it was obvious right from the outset that there had to be a link between the attacks. The death of Aidan Horan may have only served to confuse the situation but the more I thought about it, the more I felt like there was a connection. And call it instinct if you like, but the more I thought about it, the more I was convinced that Nathaniel Callaghan was behind it all. The game finally playing out. I just didn't know the rules.

'Three firearms incidents in less than twenty-four hours,' said one of the journalists, fixing Blizzard with a searching look. 'Things would seem to be spiralling out of control in your division, Chief Inspector.'

Blizzard, having taken a shower in the rest room and changed his clothes, was once again at the front of the briefing room at Abbey Road Police Station, the pictures from the night before having been removed to avoid prying journalists' eyes. Feeling even more thick-headed than before and with his temple still throbbing, the inspector sat behind the desk and stared bleakly out at the assembled newspaper and radio reporters, photographers and television crews, more than he had ever seen in the briefing room, all of them attracted by the sensational events of the past two days.

It was late afternoon and the inspector had finally, and reluctantly, ceded to the Press Office's repeated pleas for him to meet the media. The tone of the first question of the press conference already had him regretting the decision; his relationship with the media had always been fraught and he knew that many of the journalists would be relishing his discomfort, particularly given that he had turned down all their requests for interviews since the shooting of Alex Mather.

Attempting to conceal his irritation at the provocative tone of the reporter's opening question, Blizzard took a few moments to select his words before he replied.

'We are certainly concerned at what has happened,' said the inspector, trying to stay calm, 'but I would not say that the situation is spiralling out of control. Such inflammatory language does little to help the situation, I would venture to suggest.'

'Do you think there is a connection between the shootings?' asked another journalist. She glanced down at the typed sheet circulated by the Press Office. 'You have not named the man shot dead outside the hospital this afternoon but we have been told that he was Aidan Horan from the east side of the city. Can you confirm that?'

'We are not giving out the name until all members of the family have been…'

'We're going to run it in our website anyway.'

Blizzard frowned and glanced over at the Senior Press Officer who was standing by the window. Alison Curry shrugged. You made your bed, her look said.

'In which case,' said Blizzard, through pursed lips. 'Yes, I can confirm the name. As to a possible connection between the three incidents, that is certainly a major line of enquiry.'

'Have you made any arrests?' asked a radio reporter.

'No.'

'Do you expect to make any soon? I am sure the public would feel safer if they knew that you were making progress.'

Blizzard glanced over to the corner of the room where Arthur Ronald was nervously watching the proceedings unfold. A refreshed John Blizzard dealing with the media was bad enough, thought the superintendent, but an exhausted inspector under pressure from hostile questioning hardly bore thinking about. Ronald crossed his fingers behind his back as the DCI battled to retain his composure.

'This investigation is in its early stages so it would be unwise of me to comment on arrests,' said Blizzard blandly. Noticing Ronald's anxious expression and recalling his boss's request to offer reassurance, he added: 'However, we do not at this stage have any reason to believe that the wider public is at risk.'

'Even with a gunman shooting someone dead in a hospital car park?' asked a television reporter. 'Where there were plenty of members of the public?'

'Like I said, we have no reason to believe that any member of the public is at risk. We believe that this is a very specific crime.'

'That must mean you believe there *is* a connection between the shooting of Mr Horan and the attacks on your officers,' said another journalist. 'That they were specifically targeted.'

'I'm not saying that, just…'

'Do you think it is significant that these shootings have occurred at a time when crime is rising in the Western Division for the first time since you took over as head of CID?' asked a television reporter. 'Are the police losing control of the streets, Chief Inspector?'

John Blizzard glared at him, gathered his papers and stalked from the room without uttering another word. Ten minutes later, a fuming Blizzard and an unhappy Alison

Curry were sitting in the superintendent's office, the inspector eyed without much enthusiasm by Arthur Ronald.

'With all due respect, John,' said the superintendent, 'you can't just walk out on the media.'

Alison Curry nodded. Blizzard scowled.

'You saw what they were like,' he said. 'Writing the headlines before they had the story. There's no way I have to sit there and take that kind of rubbish.'

'Come on, John,' said Alison. 'We can't afford to go round alienating the media.'

'But they'd already written their sodding stories!'

'Nevertheless,' said Ronald, 'Alison is right. We need their help on this one. Can we undo some of the damage, Alison?'

'You could arrest someone,' she said. 'That would help.'

Blizzard glowered at her and resisted the urge to walk out of the room; twice in ten minutes would not look good, he decided. Instead, he tried to strike a conciliatory note. He seemed to have been doing that a lot, he thought, but he had enough enemies without making more.

'OK, I apologise for my behaviour,' he said. 'We're all under a lot of pressure and what happened to our people has shaken us up.'

'So, what do you want me to tell the media?' asked Alison. 'They'll need regular updates on this one.'

'Can you not sweet talk them?' asked Ronald.

'Sweet talking only goes so far, sir. This is a massive story, you saw how many journalists were in today, everyone from the local people to Japanese media and all their newsdesks are yelling for new angles. They are camped outside the police station.'

'OK,' said Ronald, 'so we need to give them more. Leave it with me.'

The Press Officer nodded and left the room. When she had gone, Ronald stood up and closed the door behind her.

'Will you behave?' he said. 'You're like a bull in a china shop, man. You need to be more accommodating. I've told you this before. My protection only goes so far.'

'I know, I know.'

'Besides, the media are the least of our worries. Nathaniel Callaghan has complained to the chief. Says you are asking questions about him.'

'Yeah, Nathaniel rang me.'

'How on earth did he get your number?'

'A good question, Arthur. Maybe we didn't search Eddie Gayle's drawer well enough. Maybe Eddie has all our numbers. Maybe there's a link between him and Nathaniel that we did not realise.'

'They certainly ran together in their early days on the east side,' said Ronald thoughtfully. 'But I would have said that the Callaghans are well out of Eddie Gayle's league these days.'

'Is the chief still happy to let us keep digging around?'

'He is but we need to stop the leaks. Who knows that you have been asking questions about Callaghan?'

'David Colley, Max Randall and Phil Glover. You. Oh, and one of my informants.'

'My money's on your informant running straight to Callaghan.'

'Not so sure,' said Blizzard. 'He is terrified of him. The last thing he will want is Callaghan finding out that he has been talking to me. He knows he'll end up in the Haft.'

'Which leaves who?'

Blizzard hesitated.

'Go on,' said Ronald. 'Get it said.'

'I would trust David Colley and Max Randall with my life. Just like I would with you.'

'Which leaves Phil Glover,' said Ronald.

Blizzard nodded.

'Which leaves Phil Glover,' Blizzard said. The inspector stood up. 'Time to get on top of this, I think.'

Chapter sixteen

Twenty minutes later, Blizzard was standing at the front of the briefing room at Abbey Road, a team of weary detectives and uniformed officers ranged in front of him.

'We need to make sense of this,' he said, pointing to the pictures of Alex Mather, George Killick and Aidan Horan now pinned to the board. 'It makes sense to assume that there is a connection between them.'

'Why assume that?' asked Chris Ramsey.

'It's a hell of a coincidence if there's not and I, for one, don't believe in coinc…'

'Yes, yes, we all know Blizzard's First Law but it doesn't always hold true, does it?' The detective inspector glanced down at the file resting on his knee. 'Yes, there is a connection between the attacks on Alex and Horan. Ballistics say the same gun was used but as for Killick, are we not looking at something unconnected? There's nothing to link him with Horan, as far as we know. Or to Alex Mather, for that matter. Or to the sex ring.'

'Fair point but I still say there's a conn…'

'And why,' said Ramsey, pointing to the only image from the previous evening that was on the board, 'is Eddie Gayle still up there? I know he had Alex's phone number but we've turned up nothing else to connect him to the shootings.'

'He's mixed up in this somehow,' said Blizzard. 'Him and Forrester. I can feel it.'

'Maybe we're making this too complicated,' said Ramsey. 'Maybe we're wrong trying to rope Eddie Gayle and Nathaniel Callaghan into things. Don't look so surprised, guv, everyone knows you and Dave went to see him.'

Blizzard glanced at Colley.

'He did not get it from me,' said the sergeant.

'It's the talk of the station,' said Ramsey. 'Are we after him then?'

Blizzard hesitated. 'I'm not sure I can involve any of you in this,' he said eventually. 'If it goes wrong, careers could be ended.'

'But we *are* after him?'

Blizzard nodded.

'Then I, for one, am in,' said Ramsey, his voice rising with emotion. 'Do you want to know why I believe in you and Arthur? Because you don't believe in anyone being untouchable. The Nathaniel Callaghans of this world are responsible for untold misery and we should be stopping them, not pussy-footing around.'

Blizzard looked at him in amazement; he had never heard the detective inspector so passionate. He looked at the other officers, all of whom were nodding their heads in agreement. The inspector felt a rush of affection for them.

'You're right,' said Blizzard. 'I have no idea where this is taking us but if anyone – and I mean anyone – crops up in this inquiry, even if it's the Pope, then I want them nicking.'

'That's more like it,' said Ramsey.

'However…' Blizzard's voice tailed off as Colley moved from his customary position leaning against the wall and sat down at a computer, his fingers flickering over the keyboard. Noticing everyone staring at him, the sergeant grinned and pressed a button. The printer in the corner of the room wheezed into life and he walked over to the machine, took out the printed sheet and, watched by the bemused officers, walked up to the board. Laughter rippled round the room when they saw that he had pinned up a picture of Pope Francis.

'Just in case,' he said, turning to face them.

The comment dissipated the tension of a few moments before and, as Colley returned to lean against the wall, a uniformed officer walked into the room and watched the scene in amazement.

'What the...?' he said.

'Sorry, Bob,' said Blizzard with a smile. 'A moment of madness. What can we do for you?'

'The car we think the gunman nicked after shooting at Mel has turned up,' said the officer. He glanced at Graham Ross. 'Dumped on wasteland and set on fire. Nothing much left for your crew, I am afraid, Versace.'

'Jesus, we're really thin on forensics on this one,' said Ross gloomily as the officer left the room, the levity of a few moments before having been banished.

'Which is why we have to explore all the connections,' said Blizzard, returning to the job in hand. 'Starting with Aidan Horan.'

He tapped the mugshot of a thin-faced young man with close-cropped lank black hair.

'Do we know why he was at the hospital?' he asked.

'His girlfriend is pregnant,' said Colley. 'Five and a half months. Twins, apparently. She said they were going in for a routine scan.'

'And do we know why anyone would want to kill him?'

'Beats me,' said the sergeant. 'Horan was a strictly small-time drug dealer. The mugshot was taken the last time he was arrested. Fined fifty quid for supplying dope to a couple of sixth form college students. Hardly the type to knock about with the likes of Eddie Gayle. And certainly not with Nathaniel Callaghan.'

'Yeah, he's mainly an east-side boy,' said Randall, who was sitting by the window. He glanced at Blizzard. 'In fact, he was in the pub where I was having a quick snifter after work on the night Alex was shot. Just a half of shandy, of course. My body's a temple, as you know.'

'Bloody weird religion,' said Colley.

The officers laughed but Randall did not seem to mind.

'What was Horan doing there?' asked Blizzard. He looked at Horan's picture and recalled their brief encounter at The Swan the night he met Randall.

'Pushing dope, I imagine,' said Randall. 'The Swan's one of his haunts. But David's right, he was low-level and he was certainly not wandering round with a big target stuck to his head.'

'That's what you think,' said a voice and everyone looked round to see Andy Barratt enter the room. The head of the surveillance unit looked across at Blizzard.

'How's the babby?' he asked with a smile. 'Still grizzling on like his Dad?'

Appreciating the conciliatory gesture, Blizzard thought of the snatched phone conversation he had had with Fee just before entering the briefing room.

'Yeah, not too bad now,' he said, returning the smile. 'Thanks for asking. You got something on Horan for us then?'

'Might well have.' Barratt walked to the front of the room. 'Aidan Horan may well have been low-level but he was also one of Alex Mather's snouts. There's a direct connection between the two of them.'

A low murmur ran round the room.

'This,' Barratt held up a sheet of paper, 'details how much we paid him during Alex's years undercover. Coming up for eight and a half grand when you tot it all up.'

'Now that is interesting,' said Blizzard.

'Yeah, and it gets better,' said Barratt. He looked at the picture of Eddie Gayle on the board. 'One of the criminals that Horan provided information about was your best mate. Never came to much, we all know what Gayle is like, but…' His voice tailed off and he looked closer at the board. 'Is that the Pope?'

'Sure is,' said Blizzard.

'What on earth is he doing there?'

Blizzard tapped the side of his nose conspiratorially.

'It's on a need to know basis, Andy,' he said. 'Need to know. However, if you spot him I want him lifted. Tell me more about Aidan Horan.'

'Yes, er, right,' said Barratt, giving the inspector a bemused look. 'Well, we were happy to keep slipping Horan a few quid because any intelligence we got on Eddie Gayle was likely to be better than what we had.'

'I take it Horan did help put some wrong-uns away as well, though?' asked Ramsey. 'You could waste a lot of money trying to put Eddie Gayle in prison.'

'He put a few away. Mostly small-time drug dealers and pimps. And all through intelligence he provided to Alex.' Barratt looked across at Colley with a rueful look. 'You'll be wanting another list, I imagine.'

''Fraid so,' said Colley.

'So,' said Blizzard, staring thoughtfully at the board, 'we could be back to where we started. Someone involved in a case involving both Alex Mather and Aidan Horan. Most likely drugs-related.'

'Maybe not,' said Colley, walking up the board. 'What if Eddie Gayle found out that Aidan Horan was passing information about him to Alex? I know we always say Eddie is not stupid enough to try something like killing coppers but what if Horan stumbled onto something so big that Eddie simply could not ignore it?'

'Yeah,' said Randall, a gleam in his eye. 'Like who issued the contract on George Killick.'

'I still favour the drugs angle,' said Ramsey. 'There's nothing to link Horan and Killick.'

'Fair point,' said Blizzard. 'So, what else do we know about Horan? He got a job?'

'He's a delivery driver,' said Colley. He flicked over a page in his pocket book. 'However, social security reckon he's not worked for more than three years. Not legitimately anyway. His last known kosher job was at A.T. Maynards on the Hacton Street Industrial Estate over on the east side.'

'Are you sure?' said Randall.

Colley looked at his notebook again.

'Yeah,' he said. 'Why? Is it important?'

'It just so happens that is where George Killick's son works. And, as I recall, Blizzard's First Law says never believe in coincidences.'

Blizzard traced his finger across the board, brushing against the images of Killick and Horan then slowly and deliberately drawing an imaginary line towards Eddie Gayle. He turned to face the officers and beamed.

'What did I say?' he said. 'Connections, always connections. Check it out, will you, David?'

Ramsey leaned over to the officer sitting next to him.

'He'll be insufferable now,' he whispered.

'I heard that,' said Blizzard.

His mobile phone rang. He took the call.

'It's Sammy B,' said a voice. 'Might have something for you. Meet me down by the river.'

Chapter seventeen

'Yeah, I know Aidan Horan, alright,' said the bespectacled grey-haired man in the overalls, stepping back from the grubby white van on which he had been working.

Bob Maynard wiped his hands on an oily rag and surveyed Colley and Detective Constable Sarah Allatt as they stood at the entrance to the cluttered workshop, which was growing gloomier and colder by the minute as the late afternoon light faded. An ageing transistor radio in the corner of the workshop struggled its way through a Beach Boys song.

'What's he done?' he asked. 'I'm not surprised he's in trouble, mind, a right bad 'un he was.'

'In what way, Mr Maynard?' asked Allatt, a slim brunette dressed in jeans and a black pullover beneath her jacket.

'Bad timekeeping. Unreliable.' Maynard shook his head. 'Cost me money in the end. I had clients ringing up asking where he was all the time. I sacked him. Had to.'

'Can't have unreliable drivers in your game,' said Colley.

'You done a bit of driving yourself then, son?'

‘Er, no,’ said the sergeant. He glanced at Allatt and gave the slightest of smiles. ‘Just took a wild guess.’

Allatt grinned.

‘Aye, well, it wasn’t just the time-keeping that made me sack him,’ said Maynard. He climbed into the driver’s seat of the van and turned the key in the ignition. The engine coughed and spluttered and gave a feeble wheeze before falling silent. ‘Bloody thing.’

Allatt stepped back and read the number plate.

‘I’m not surprised, Bob, it must be thirty years old,’ she said. ‘No wonder it’s knackered.’

‘We’ll get her running, pet, plenty more miles in her yet.’ Maynard jumped out, went round to the open bonnet. ‘Hand me that spanner, will you, young lady?’

The detective picked up the tool from a nearby workbench.

‘Try the alternator,’ she said as she handed it over. She noticed Colley’s raised eyebrow. ‘Dad ran stock car racers for years. I grew up in garages. So, Mr Maynard, what was the other reason you sacked Aidan Horan?’

‘It was mainly the folks he attracted,’ said Maynard’s voice echoing from under the bonnet. ‘Some real rum ’uns came to see him. It was making the girls in the office uneasy. Tell the truth, it was making me uneasy, an’ all and I don’t scare easy. You see all sorts in this game, I can tell you.’

‘Did you know that Aidan was selling drugs?’ asked Colley.

‘No, but I reckoned he was up to something dodgy. And money kept disappearing from the office.’ Maynard emerged from beneath the bonnet. ‘Why are you so interested in Aidan anyway? He hasn’t worked here for three or four years.’

‘He’s been murdered,’ said Colley. ‘Shot dead earlier this afternoon.’

'Was he that bloke at the hospital?' said Maynard with a low whistle. 'I heard summat on the radio but didn't know it was him.'

'Well, it's him alright.' Colley pulled copies of the pictures showing Eddie Gayle and Ronnie Forrester out of his jacket pocket and held them up for Maynard to see. 'You ever seen these guys before? They ever visit Aidan here?'

'Not him,' said Maynard, pointing to Eddie Gayle with a grimy, oil-streaked hand. 'Never seen him but the other one, he used to come to see Aidan. They were thick as thieves. It was when he started turning up that I fired him. Scary fella. Something about his eyes. Looked right through you.'

'Did you ever hear what they were talking about?' asked Allatt.

'No, and I didn't want to neither.' Maynard disappeared back beneath the bonnet. 'I don't get involved in nothing like that.'

'Very wise,' said Colley, slipping the pictures back into his pocket. 'Very wise indeed. Tell me, did Aidan Horan know Barrie Killick? I believe Barrie's one of your drivers?'

Maynard re-emerged from beneath the bonnet.

'Aidan was before his time,' he said. Maynard jumped back into the cab and turned the ignition key. The engine coughed into life.

'See?' said Maynard, grinning at Allatt. 'I told you she'd be alright.'

'Any time,' said the detective constable.

***

Blizzard guided his car along the rough track cutting through the wasteland which spread out from the city centre. Reaching a grassy area just metres from the river bank, he cut the engine and got out. Walking over to the river, he stared out over the murky brown waters.

Water had always had a soothing effect on his mind, allowing it to settle and clear itself of clutter, and turning up his coat collar against the biting wind and the icy spray that drove off the river, the inspector stood in silent contemplation for a few moments, turning the events of the past forty-eight hours over and over in his mind. It had been a frustrating time with dead-end after dead-end yet the inspector retained the belief that he was just one piece of information away from putting it all together. If he could just reach out far enough, the answer would be his. He could not help feeling that he had missed something, that someone had said something during the past two days of which he should have taken more notice.

The sound of someone approaching along the path along the river broke into his reverie and he saw his informant Sammy B emerge through the trees. He looked frightened.

'Didn't think I'd see you for a long time,' said Blizzard. He noticed the way Sammy's eyes were darting from left to right, constantly seeking confirmation that they were alone. 'Jesus, you look terrified.'

'I am,' said Sammy B. He walked up close to the inspector and lowered his voice. 'There's some heavy stuff going down.'

'Then tell me because I'm going nuts trying to work it out.'

'There's things you don't know about the murder of that drug dealer over at the hospital,' said Sammy B.

'We're thinking it may be linked to the death of George Killick. Or maybe something to do with Eddie Gayle?'

'You're not far off. Word is that Aidan Horan had something on Ronnie Forrester.'

Blizzard's eyes gleamed.

'Now what,' he said, 'might Aidan Horan know about that sleaze-ball?'

Sammy B glanced round again.

'You got to promise on your life that you did not hear this from me,' he said. 'Cross these people and you've seen what happens. Ronnie Forrester is out of control and it ain't no coincidence that your mate Mather and Aidan Horan got themselves shot.'

'I'm listening.'

'The word is that Aidan Horan was passing information about Ronnie to Alex Mather. Forrester got to hear about it and panicked. The gunman is working for him.'

'Do you know who the gunman is?'

Sammy shook his head. 'No one does. Someone new. The word is Ronnie knows him from way back.'

'Do you know what kind of information Aidan Horan was passing on to Alex?'

'I can guess.' Sammy B looked round again, searching the wasteland for signs of movement but nothing stirred among the derelict buildings, rotting pallets and coils of rusting wire. 'I heard that Ronnie wants to be a Mr Big and is bringing in a delivery of guns to sell them to some hot-heads from London. Political types. Eddie wants nothing to do with it. He's trying to talk him out of it.'

'What, Eddie Gayle upholding the law?'

'Nothing so noble,' said Sammy B. 'See, these hot-heads normally deal with Nathaniel Callaghan. Ronnie's trying to set himself up against the Callaghans and Eddie's terrified that when Nathaniel finds out he'll think he's involved. If you ain't careful, you'll have a bloodbath on your hands.'

And with that, Sammy B scuttled away in the gathering afternoon shadows.

Blizzard's mobile rang.

'No rest for the wicked,' he sighed, taking the call. 'David, what you got?'

'Not sure,' said Colley's voice, 'but I think we might be getting closer to Ronnie Forrester.'

'You have no idea,' said Blizzard, walking back to his car.

* * *

Twenty minutes later, Blizzard was heading along the corridor towards Arthur Ronald's office at Abbey Road, whistling as he went. On entering the room, he stood and watched in bemusement as the superintendent fussed around a pot plant on the windowsill.

'What on earth are you doing?' asked the inspector.

'Earth's the word,' said the superintendent. He did not turn round but continued to ferret around in the plant. 'This needs a spot of compost.'

'What?'

'See, every time you walk into my office, particularly when you're whistling, it takes me a step closer to enforced early retirement so the missus has been saying for a while that I need a hobby for when it happens.' Ronald turned round. 'She's trying to get me interested in gardening. I said no – there's no fuchsia in it.'

'You and Colley should go on the stage together,' said Blizzard. He took a seat and watched as his friend moved over to the kettle. 'Besides, what's to say this is not just a social visit from an old friend asking after your health?'

'Because,' said Ronald. He reached for the teabags then turned to look at his friend, 'I know that look only too well. It says you fancy a bit of devilment.'

'Who, me?' Blizzard tried to look innocent.

'Yes, you.' Ronald sat down and gave Blizzard a rueful look. 'What is it this time? Callaghan? Eddie Gayle?'

'Ronnie Forrester,' said Blizzard. 'I think he's behind the shootings. I want to put him under surveillance and I want you to keep Organised Crime off my back.'

'A trowel would be nice,' said Ronald, standing up as the kettle started to boil. 'A gold-plated one, maybe.'

'Nice for what?'

'My retirement present.'

'Who says you're getting a present?' replied Blizzard.

* * *

Sitting behind the wheel of the car as darkness fell, the gunman knew, as weariness began to assail him in the gathering gloom, that he was out of control. That fatigue and adrenaline had combined to create a heady cocktail. He found himself liking the sensation.

Having stolen the Ford Fiesta from the city centre following the shooting of Aidan Horan at the hospital, he had driven beyond the eastern fringes of Hafton and out towards the east coast, casting wary glances at the numerous police patrol vehicles that he passed. Now, after leaving the city far behind, he turned off the main road into a deserted lane and started to relax. Parking up near a straggly wind-blown copse, he sat as the winter afternoon light began to fade and tried to make sense of what was happening to him.

As he did so, he realised that murdering Aidan Horan had changed everything, had flicked a switch which had triggered dark thoughts the likes of which he had never experienced before. He was a killer now. At first, the feeling of euphoria had surprised him. Even after he had gunned down Alex Mather and fired at the officer in Waterston Lane, the man had still felt nervous, uneasy, disconnected from the gun. However, killing Horan had infused him with a new confidence, given him a sense of release and a desire to kill again.

He was also experiencing a sense that he was untouchable. Had he not driven freely round the city without being caught? And even when the police had stopped him, had he not forced them away? Counselling himself to retain his caution, the man reached over and opened the glove compartment to survey the gun. As he did so, his mobile phone rang. He pulled the device out of his jacket pocket and took the call.

'Where are you?' asked Forrester.

'Parked up over towards the coast.'

'What the fuck are you doing there?'

'Keeping out of the way,' said the gunman. 'I take it you heard that Horan is dead?'

'Yeah. Just don't delay too long finishing the job. When do you plan to kill Blizzard?'

'Tomorrow. I was thinking of laying low for a while. I've not had much sleep and there's a cheap bed and breakfast in Sleacombe.'

'I said I wanted …'

'The roads in the city are crawling with police,' said the man. 'Sleacombe is deserted out of season. There's no one in the caravans and most of the cottages are holiday lets so they're empty.'

'Actually, it might not be a bad idea,' said the voice. 'There's certainly a lot of police activity. But don't forget, I want Blizzard dead as soon as possible.'

'And Mather? What if he comes round?'

'You leave Alex Mather to me.'

The call ended and the man sat back in his seat and closed his eyes. After a few minutes in which he felt himself drifting into slumber, he snapped his eyes open, turned the ignition key and, as the winter afternoon light continued to fade, guided the vehicle in the direction of Sleacombe.

Chapter eighteen

It was shortly after 8pm when fatigue finally drove John Blizzard from Abbey Road. As he guided his car through the light mid-evening traffic, he decided to ignore his pounding head and stop off at the hospital, pausing briefly in the car park to talk to the officer standing guard at the spot where Aidan Horan had fallen. It was the same young constable he had seen watching over Mather's cottage two nights before.

'You do get all the best jobs,' said Blizzard as he approached the young officer, who was stamping his feet to keep warm in the biting chill of the night. 'Anything interesting?'

'The same press photographer, sir. Sent him on his way.'

'Good lad.'

'How's DC Mather, sir?'

'Hanging in there, son, hanging in there.'

Five minutes later, the inspector was on the third floor of the hospital.

'How is he?' he asked as he walked into the intensive care unit to see Rachel sitting on a chair next to her brother's bed.

She did not reply and he noticed that her eyes were closed. Blizzard stood for a few moments and wondered whether or not he should let her sleep but, as he turned away, she stirred.

'I must have dropped off,' she mumbled.

'Sorry I woke you,' said Blizzard. 'Any news?'

'The doctors are still not saying much,' said Rachel, sitting up and glancing at the clock on the wall. 'He's still critically ill. It seems a long time ago that I found him.'

'I know how you feel.' Blizzard pulled up a chair. 'Have you remembered anything else that may help us?'

'I wish I had. The nurses said that there was a shooting in the car park. Was that anything to do with Alex?'

'Not sure yet,' said the inspector. 'Does the name Aidan Horan mean anything to you?'

'Is that the man who died?'

He nodded.

'Sorry,' she said. 'I have never heard of him. I'm afraid I've not been much help to you, Chief Inspector.'

'Don't worry about it. You and I move in somewhat different circles, I think. I'd be worried if you did know that type of people.'

'There's certainly not as much excitement in the world of travel agents,' she said with a smile. 'This has given me a whole new insight into Alex's world and made me realise how little people know about what happens in their city. I certainly had no idea.'

'Probably just as well,' said Blizzard. 'Better to let us worry about the slime-balls.'

'Well, I for one appreciate what you do.' She noticed the darkening beneath the detective's eyes. 'You look exhausted.'

'I am. I just popped in on my way home.'

'Are you married?'

'We live together. She's a detective constable.'

'At least she understands the risks you run. You got any kids?'

'One. He's only a few weeks old. Fee's on maternity leave.'

'Just what you need when you're working all hours, a baby.'

'Yeah,' he said, giving her a rueful look. 'You're not wrong there.'

'Have you ever thought about packing it all in? Being a dad is a big responsibility. What would happen to your son if some harm befell you like it did Alex?'

'We've discussed it,' said Blizzard. 'Fee says the last thing she wants is me kicking around the house. Says it would drive both of us mad.'

Rachel glanced over at her unconscious brother.

'Polly tried a couple of times,' she said. 'Tried to persuade Alex to quit and find another job but he wouldn't. Said it would drive him mad as well. Besides, what else can an undercover detective do?'

Blizzard thought back to his conversation with Mather on the day he was shot.

'Actually, I think he was coming round to the idea,' he said. 'Maybe packing it all in and finding something else.'

'Maybe that's what he told you but he'll not do it. You're both the same, you're wedded to your job, both of you.'

'That's what my first wife used to say. She never understood.' Blizzard stood up, fished in his jacket pocket and handed her a business card. 'I'm going home now but if you need anything just ring. Doesn't matter what time. I'll probably be up with the baby anyway.'

The inspector did not leave the hospital immediately because a sudden craving for sweet tea sent him to the ground floor cafe. The inspector sat for twenty minutes, deep in thought as he sipped his drink, with the result that he did not depart until shortly before 9pm. As he was in the corridor leading from the cafe, his mobile phone rang.

'It's David,' said the sergeant. 'Sorry to disturb you but there's something you need to know. Where are you?'

'At the hospital. Been to see Alex.'

'And?'

'No change.'

'Well, be warned, the surveillance team say that Forrester has just pulled into the hospital car park. Do you want me to call in the armed boys and gals?'

'Is he alone?'

'Yeah.'

'Not sure they can get here quickly enough if he is going to try something. Besides, we've still got an armed guard on the ward. I'll keep an eye out for him.'

'OK. Be careful.'

As the inspector walked towards the front entrance, he caught a glimpse of Forrester pushing his way through the double-doors at the far end of the corridor. The inspector instinctively ducked into a side room before Forrester could see him. Once Forrester had passed by, Blizzard peered round the door and saw him walk towards the lifts, tailed at a distance by one of Andy Barratt's surveillance team.

One of the lift doors slid open and out stepped Rachel Mather. The inspector continued to watch as she glanced round to make sure that she was not being observed then greeted Forrester with the merest of touches on the hand. Their conversation did not last long, just a matter of seconds, then Rachel walked back into the lift. As Forrester headed back towards the main entrance, Blizzard shrunk back into the shadows of the room. Once Forrester had passed by, Blizzard poked his head out and watched his retreating back.

'Well, well,' he murmured, 'maybe Chris is right. Maybe we are making this more complicated than it needs to be.'

The inspector edged his way to the hospital entrance and watched as Forrester skirted round the wooded edge of the car park so that the young constable did not see him. Glancing round nervously, Forrester got into a black saloon and drove away. An unmarked police car eased into position behind him, keeping its distance so as not to arouse suspicion.

As they disappeared from view, the inspector rang Colley.

'Everything OK?' asked the sergeant. 'I've got an armed car on its way. It'll be there in a couple of minutes.'

'No need, he's gone.'

'You alright? You sound weird.'

'I have a sick feeling in the pit of my stomach,' said Blizzard. 'I've just seen Forrester with someone he shouldn't be with in a million years. I know you want to get home but can you do a check for me?'

After finishing his call, the inspector walked across the car park, nodded at the young constable and was just unlocking his vehicle's door when his mobile rang.

'You coming home?' said a woman's voice.

'Yes,' he said wearily. 'On my way.'

* * *

Twenty-five minutes later, the inspector was sitting in his favourite armchair in his living room and sipping another cup of strong tea with three sugars, made by Fee. They had been together for more than three years. Neither had made a conscious decision to move in together but, once she had become pregnant, she had spent virtually all her time there and Blizzard, a loner before he took up with her, had found himself constantly surprised by his growing domestic instincts. He looked fondly at the young blonde detective constable, who was sitting on the sofa, cradling a mug of coffee.

'You OK then?' he asked.

'Yes, not too bad, love. Not sure about you, though. You look done in.'

'I am.' Blizzard glanced across the room to where baby Michael slumbered in his cot. 'You must be exhausted as well, mind.'

'Actually, I don't feel too bad,' she said, sipping her coffee. 'Jay came over after school when David told her how bad things had got so I grabbed a bit of sleep. She brought Laura and that seemed to cheer Michael up, then he dropped off to sleep just before they left.'

'He certainly looks more settled,' said Blizzard, glancing at the cot. 'The little mite must be shattered.'

'Not too bad now. How's Alex? I heard that it's touch and go.'

'It is, I am afraid. I talked to his sister and...'

'He's got a sister?' said Fee. 'I didn't know that. How is she?'

'Holding on in there.' Blizzard decided to play it straight and not divulge his inner thoughts. It wouldn't do to voice things that might have an innocent explanation. He gave a slight frown; how could this be innocent?

'I heard that Aidan Horan got shot?' said Fee. 'I arrested him, you know.'

'You did?'

'Remember when I did my six-month stint with the Drugs Squad on the east side? He'd sold drugs to a couple of teenagers at a college disco. Cannabis, as I recall.'

'What was he like?'

'Normal guy really. Certainly not the type you'd expect to get himself shot, that's for sure. Strictly small-time. What was he doing at the hospital?'

'His girlfriend's pregnant. Twins. They were going for a scan.'

'Poor girl,' said Fee. She looked across to the cot as the baby stirred then settled down again. 'A baby losing a father just does not bear thinking about.'

'You're the second person who's reminded me of that tonight.'

Fee hesitated and silence settled on the room for a few moments.

'Will they come after anyone else?' she asked eventually. 'I mean, first Alex then Aidan Horan.'

He looked at her. 'Meaning am I on their list?'

She nodded. 'Yes, are you on the list?'

Blizzard gave her a reassuring smile.

'Nothing to worry about,' he said.

But he was worried. Later that night, as he lay in bed, Fee breathing gently as she slept next to him and the baby mercifully slumbering in his cot in the corner of the room, Blizzard stared up at the ceiling, eyes wide open as he let the memories play out. Memories of Alex Mather, of Eddie Gayle, of Ronnie Forrester and of a dead girl dying in a squalid B & B with a needle hanging out of her arm.

Quietly, the inspector got out of bed and padded across to stare through the gap in the curtains. The road was deserted. He sighed and went back to bed. Bloody paranoia, he thought bleakly, a gift from Alex Mather. Sleep, when it did come, heralded dreams in which the only face he could see was Nathaniel Callaghan's calm stare across a massive mahogany desk, just the faintest hint of a smile playing on his thin lips.

Chapter nineteen

Just after 6am, the baby awoke and Blizzard was roused from his disturbed dreams. Feeling thick-headed, he got slowly out of bed, wincing as his back gave a twinge sending shards of pain shooting up his spine.

'I'll do his breakfast,' he murmured.

'You're a star,' said Fee and rolled over.

Blizzard walked gingerly down the stairs with the child in his arms, relieved that the pain from his back was easing, and headed for the kitchen where he heated up a bottle. Once that was done, the inspector took Michael through into the living room, switched on the television and flicked to the news channel, which he watched as he fed the baby. When the local news came on, the lead story was about the death of Aidan Horan and the picture switched to Arthur Ronald standing outside Abbey Road Police Station in late afternoon light.

'Go get 'em,' Arthur,' said Blizzard, looking at the empty bottle. 'Boy, you were hungry, little one.'

'We are investigating a number of new leads following the murder of Mr Horan,' Ronald said into the camera in his most solemn voice, 'and we are making progress in our hunt for the man who shot him. I would urge people to stay calm. We have received a number of calls from worried members of the public concerned that they may be at risk but we do not believe that they are in any danger. It is the firm belief of DCI Blizzard and his investigation team that the death of Mr Horan and the attacks on our police officers are connected and that the wider public need not worry.'

The wider public, thought Blizzard, what do they know anyway? Rachel Mather's words from the previous evening came back to the inspector as he cradled his now sleeping child. *This has given me a whole new insight into Alex's world and made me realise how little people know about what happens in the city. I certainly had no idea.*

'I'll bet you didn't,' said Blizzard quietly.

He turned down the volume on the television and reached over to where his mobile phone had been charging on a table, moving slowly so as not to disturb the slumbering baby. He dialled Colley's number. When the call was answered, the inspector could hear the theme tune of Thomas the Tank Engine playing in the background.

'Thank God you've rung,' said the sergeant. 'Boy, have I got news for you. The Fat Controller is going to be livid.'

'What, Arthur?' asked a bewildered inspector. 'Why's he going to be angry?'

'Get with the programme, man,' said Colley. 'James the red engine has lost a wheel after bumping into Thomas in the shed and it looks like he's going to collide with the water tower. Eat some more yoghurt, Laura, there's a good girl.'

'Bloody hell,' said Blizzard, 'ten past six and you're cracking jokes.'

'I thank you,' said Colley. 'I take it you are ringing about Rachel Mather?'

'I am afraid so. You got anything?'

'Got some stuff emailed overnight. Look, are you sure about this, guv? I mean, the woman's brother is lying in hospital fighting for his life. Good news, James has missed the water tower. And I was right, the Fat Controller is furious. Come to think of it, he does look like Arthur when he's mad. Something about the way the eyes narrow. Anyway, are we really saying that Rachel might be tied up in this somehow?'

'I know what I saw, David.'

Colley sighed. 'Aye, I imagine you do. Well, for what it's worth, she may have motive. Time for one of your wise sayings, methinks. The one about going where the evidence takes you, perhaps? Or how about: "it's always the ones nearest to you that you have to worry about"?'

'Either will do. So, what do we have on her? She got previous?'

'No, nothing like that.' Blizzard heard the rustling of papers. 'Not unless you count the fact that she recently got stopped for speeding.'

'We've all been stopped for speeding. So, where's the motive for trying to kill her brother?'

'Ah, well, that's where it gets interesting.' Colley rustled another piece of paper. 'You know she said that George Killick handled the sale of the house when she and her husband got divorced?'

'Yeah.'

'Well, turns out it had to be a rush job because hubby was buggering off to live in New Zealand with a sheep he met in a nightclub.' The sergeant paused. 'That's a joke.'

'I'll take your word for it. What's the sale of the house got to do with anything?'

'Well... it's Uncle John, lovey; yes, Michael's Daddy – well, the husband demanded his money immediately. He'd landed a job in New Zealand and needed to get over there quickly.'

'So?'

'So, they lost money on the house despite Killick's best efforts. Quite a bit, actually. Close to six figures. What's more, I pulled a favour from a mate of mine who works in bank security. Rachel may have said that she works in a travel agents but the pay cheques stopped six months ago. I'm going to see her boss this morning but one thing's for certain, Rachel Mather is deeply in debt.'

'So, she'd do anything for money?'

'Not sure anyone would go as far as to kill their brother, guv. Money or not.'

'You have such a trusting nature.'

'Time for your saying on everyone being capable of doing anything if the need is there?'

'Sometimes,' said Blizzard, shifting in his chair as his back twinged, 'I do not think I get the respect I deserve but let's say we give her the benefit of the doubt, it is still true that Rachel Mather and Forrester know each other. And whatever Forrester wanted to say to her last night, it was important enough to risk visiting the hospital.'

'Fair point,' said Colley. He was silent for a few moments. 'One that's enough to well and truly piss off the Fat Controller.'

Blizzard heard the Thomas the Tank Engine music in the background and sighed.

'Sometimes, I hate my job,' he said.

'Yeah, me too. See why I don't want to be promoted to inspector? So where now?'

'I think,' said Blizzard, 'that it's time to set a little trap.'

When the call had ended, the inspector looked down at the baby sleeping peacefully on his lap. Something about the child's innocence moved him, as it so often did, and he wondered, not for the first time, if it was fair to bring a child into such a cruel world.

***

The ringing of her mobile phone shook Rachel Mather out of a deep sleep shortly after seven. Having been sent home from the hospital by one of the nurses the previous night because she was exhausted, Rachel had been to see her son at his grandmother's and had then gone home where she had fallen asleep on the sofa. Now, bleary-eyed, she struggled to work out where she was for a few moments then reached for the phone, which was lying on a table next to a cup of coffee that had long since gone cold.

'Hello,' she said.

'It's Sister Maitland,' said a woman's voice. 'Sorry to ring so early but I thought I'd let you know that your brother has taken a turn for the worse. I think you'd better come in. We're not sure how much time he has.'

'Thank you,' said Rachel. Ending the call, she dialled another number. 'Ronnie, I've just heard from the hospital. They say he's dying.'

'Good,' said Forrester. 'That just leaves Blizzard.'

* * *

Back in intensive care, the nurse looked unhappily at Arthur Ronald and Detective Constable Sarah Allatt, then at the slim dark-haired woman standing beside Alex Mather's bed.

'I don't like doing this, Mrs Mather,' said Nurse Maitland. 'Your husband is on the mend so telling his sister otherwise goes against everything I believe in.'

'My sister-in-law,' said Polly in a clipped tone of voice, 'didn't even try to find me when Alex was shot. It was only through Superintendent Ronald here that I found out what had happened.'

The nurse still looked uneasy.

'Look, I appreciate your reservations,' said Ronald. 'And we wouldn't ask unless it was necessary.'

'It's highly irregular and…'

'Let me level with you, Sister,' said Ronald. 'We have reason to believe that another attempt may be made on Alex's life and that Rachel may be the one to do it.'

The nurse looked shocked. 'Surely not,' she said. 'I mean, Rachel has hardly left her brother's side. She only went home last night because we told her to.'

'I sincerely hope we are wrong but if she thinks that Alex will not regain consciousness then he will be safer. The doctor says that the extra sedation won't do him any harm.'

Nurse Maitland shook her head.

'It must be a wicked world you live in to make you so suspicious,' she said. 'This has made me realise how little people know about what happens in the city. I certainly had no idea.'

'Most people don't,' murmured Ronald.

* * *

It was just before 9.30 when Colley entered the travel agents and walked up to the receptionist, flashing his warrant card.

'Detective Sergeant Colley from Abbey Road Police Station,' he said. 'I rang earlier. Is Mr Baines in?'

The girl picked up the desk phone and moments later the sergeant was ushered into a back room to be met by a fussy-looking balding man.

'I am Leonard Baines,' said the man, extending hand. 'I am not sure I am happy to talk about personal details of staff members. What's…'

'I appreciate that,' said Colley, taking the proffered seat, 'but I would not ask if it was not necessary. Lives may be at stake.'

'I see.' Baines considered the comment for a few moments. 'It might help if I knew what it was about.'

'I'd rather not say.'

'Is it about that police officer who was shot?' asked Baines. 'Rachel has a brother in the police force.'

'It may be linked, yes. How long did Rachel work for you?'

'She had been with us for fourteen years. A model employee until about six months ago. Then she met *him*.'

Colley reached into his jacket pocket and fished out a picture of Ronnie Forrester, which he showed to the travel agent.

'Not him, by any chance?' he said.

'Yes, that's him. Nasty piece of work. Scary eyes. After she met him, she changed. Started coming in late, taking days off when she said she was sick although she was seen out with him on at least two occasions.'

'So, you sacked her?'

'I didn't want to, Sergeant, she had been a good worker but when he started coming into the office, I had no option. He was frightening my other staff and I could not have that.'

Colley nodded.

'He can have that effect on people,' said the sergeant.

'Can I ask why you are so interested in them?'

'You don't want to know,' said Colley, standing up, 'You really don't.'

* * *

'Come on, son,' said Blizzard, staring across the table at an uneasy Mark Roberts. 'A man dies in your cell and you hear nothing?'

'Yeah, that's right.'

Blizzard shook his head.

'I don't buy it, Mark,' he said. 'I don't buy it at all.'

It was half past nine and Blizzard and Randall were sitting in one of the interview rooms at Hafton Prison, the atmosphere rank with the sweat of the inmate, who eyed them with growing anxiety, disturbed by their grim expressions.

'You going to tell us the truth?' asked Blizzard.

'I have done. It's what happened. I heard nowt.' Roberts gave a wicked smile. 'I'm a heavy sleeper.'

'Heavy sleeper or not, I reckon you'd have heard a man breathing his last, Mark.'

'Yeah, well I didn't.'

Blizzard did not reply but instead read a piece of paper lying on the desk. He did so slowly, allowing the pressure to build on Roberts as he anxiously watched the inspector.

'I see you got three years for burglary,' said the inspector, finally looking up. 'You've only got six months to go.'

'So?'

'So, I don't understand why you would give all that up to kill someone like George Killick.'

'What do you mean kill him?' said Roberts, sweat glistening on his brow and fear starting in his eyes. 'They told me died of natural causes.'

'It depends if you think it's natural to suffocate a man with a pillow. But like I say, I can't understand why you would do it. Give it long enough and someone else would have done it anyway. We all know how they view child abusers in places like these. Or the man himself would have done it. From what we hear, he was on the edge anyway.'

'But he died of a heart attack.'

'Ah, if only it were that simple, Mark,' said Randall. 'He was murdered and you know it.'

'Well, I didn't do nothing to him.'

'The post-mortem suggests otherwise,' said Blizzard. 'And since you were the only person in the cell with him the night he died, you don't have to be Sherlock Holmes to work out what happened.'

Blizzard glanced at Randall.

'Can't see either of us picking up a judge's commendation for solving this one, can you, Max?' he said. 'All pretty straightforward, I would say.'

Randall nodded.

'I guess so,' he said. 'What do you reckon, charge him now? Life, that is. What's he now. Twenty-eight? I reckon he could be at least fifty when he comes out. Longer if he continues to play silly buggers and denies it.'

'Now, you listen…' began Roberts, sitting forward and jabbing a finger at Blizzard.

'No, you listen,' said Blizzard, an edge in his voice now. 'You are in big trouble, Mark. We could charge you with murder now, save a lot of time. We don't need you to say anything. But what I want to know is who put you up to it? There's no way that killing George Killick was your idea. As far as we can gather, you did not even know the man.'

'Yeah, so why would I kill him then?' Roberts sat back and folded his arms. 'Answer me that. Anyway, I ain't saying nothing until my lawyer arrives.'

'Ah, yes, your lawyer.' Blizzard gave Randall a knowing smile. 'That should be interesting.'

He glanced down at another piece of paper on the desk.

'I see, you've had some interesting visitors the last few days,' he said. 'Eddie Gayle. Ronnie Forrester. Yet there's nothing in your file to suggest that you know them either. What did they want with you, I wonder?'

Roberts shook his head.

'I ain't saying nothing,' he said.

'Then let me save you the trouble and tell you what I think happened,' said Blizzard, leaning forward. 'See, we know that DCI Glover was talking to George Killick about giving up the man who ran the sex ring. I think that person wanted Killick silenced before he could talk and I think someone picked you. I think Eddie Gayle was told to make sure you got the job done.'

Before Roberts could reply, the door opened and in walked a tall, elegant man dressed in a smart grey suit topped off with a floral buttonhole.

'Leonard Maskell, as I live and breathe,' said Blizzard, eying the lawyer with faint amusement as he took his seat. 'I wondered when you would show up.'

'I take it,' said the solicitor, unclipping his briefcase, 'that you have not charged my client yet?'

'Your client?' said Blizzard. 'Bit low-brow for you, isn't he? I thought you represented the esteemed representatives of the professional classes. No, we have not charged him. Not yet anyway. Although it will not be long. Max was just licking the end of his pencil.'

'Then I would like to request that I have some time with him before we proceed.'

'I think you'll need it,' said Blizzard and the detectives left the room.

'You were right about Leonard Maskell,' said Randall in delight as they walked along the corridor. 'You said he'd be mixed up in this somehow. How many of the sex ring did he represent?'

'Four, as I recall. The accountant from Fife Street, the one who ran the recruitment company in the city centre, that architect from Hatcham and our esteemed Mr Killick. And he represents Nathaniel Callaghan. We're close, Max. Really close. Time to close the net, I think.'

'Go for it, matey.'

They walked further along the corridor and Blizzard made a call on his mobile.

'Andy,' he said, talking in a low voice as Randall leaned closer to hear the conversation. 'Did the tap on Leonard Maskell's phone work?'

'Sure did,' said the head of surveillance. 'What time did the prison let Roberts know that you were coming to see him?'

'Just after eight.'

'Yes, well, ten minutes later Roberts called a number that our tech guys have traced to a mobile that Nathaniel Callaghan is known to use. The prison officers have found the mobile hidden in Roberts' cell so we know he made the call. Then Callaghan called Leonard Maskell.'

'Got him!' exclaimed Randall, clapping a hand to his mouth on realising that he had spoken too loudly.

The interview room door opened and the solicitor appeared, eying the detectives suspiciously. He motioned to them and the detectives followed him back into the room.

'What evidence do you have against my client?' asked Maskell as they sat down. 'Surely it is all circumstantial.'

'Maybe so but the post-mortem says he was murdered and they were locked in a cell together for nine hours,' said Blizzard. 'According to the prison officers, no one else went into the room. I imagine that would be enough for any jury. I mean, he wasn't killed by the tooth fairy, was he?'

'Indeed not,' said the solicitor. He glanced at Roberts. 'It seems that we have very little manoeuvring room, Chief Inspector.'

'I'd agree with that.'

'Then my client will plead guilty.'

Roberts closed his eyes but said nothing.

'That easy?' said Blizzard. 'No attempt to dispute the evidence?'

'I do not see that I have any option, Chief Inspector. As you quite rightly point out, no jury in the land would acquit him.'

'So, why did he do it?' asked Blizzard.

'My client has a long-standing distaste for child abusers,' said Maskell. 'I am sure that you, as a new father, can appreciate that, Chief Inspector. When they were placed in a cell together, it became too much for him. He snapped and...'

'Try again,' said Blizzard, wondering how Maskell knew that he had a baby. For a few seconds, he battled the rising sense of panic.

'It's the truth,' said Maskell. He seemed confident. Sure of himself. In control. 'My client has two children aged six and nine, the same age as some of the sex ring's victims. He found himself repulsed by what George Killick had done, lost his temper and killed him in a fit of rage.'

'I very much doubt that it was a spur of the moment thing,' said Blizzard. 'For a start, we know that George

Killick started talking to DCI Glover just over a fortnight ago. He offered to give up the name of the man behind the sex ring in return for time off his sentence.'

'My client knows nothing about that.'

'I think he knows all about that. Then lo and behold, Mark here, who has never been a violent man, assaults another inmate and gets himself placed in the special protection wing where he gets put in a cell with George Killick. Just a day after receiving a visit from Eddie Gayle and his knuckle-head pal Ronnie Forrester, I might add.'

'A nice story, Chief Inspector,' said Maskell, 'and all fiction. My client will not be changing his account of what hap…'

'Do you know what I think?' said Blizzard. 'I think the man who put the money up to kill George Killick was your esteemed client Nathaniel Callaghan.'

The lawyer looked worried for the first time since he had walked into the room.

'I do not think we have to involve that man,' he said. 'Nathaniel Callaghan has nothing to do with this.'

'Ah, but I think we do have to involve him. I think you have come here not for Mark's sake but to ensure that he knows to keep quiet about Nathaniel Callaghan. What was the deal, cough to murder, serve his time and no one kills him? Or more likely, no one harms his family?'

Roberts looked anxious.

'You have no evidence to…' began Maskell.

'Do you know what this is?' asked Blizzard, reaching into his jacket pocket and withdrawing a piece of paper. 'This is a list of your phone calls this morning, Mr Maskell. It's amazing what people will do when they think no one is watching.'

Rendered temporarily speechless, Maskell stared in horror at the piece of paper.

'See,' continued Blizzard, glancing down at the print-out, 'you received a call from Nathaniel Callaghan this morning a matter of minutes after Mark rang him to say that we were coming to interview him. And here you are. Right on cue.'

'This is an outrage!' exclaimed the lawyer, recovering from his shock and finding his voice, but both detectives could see that behind the bluster lurked fear.

'Outrage or not, you're in this up to your neck,' said Blizzard. 'As is Nathaniel Callaghan. See, we don't believe that anyone is untouchable.'

The lawyer stood up.

'I would have said we are done here,' he said icily.

'I think *you* are,' said Blizzard. He looked at Roberts. 'Mark, do you want him to go?'

Roberts hesitated.

'I would strongly recommend…' began Maskell.

'You strongly recommended that he plead guilty to murder, no questions asked,' said Blizzard. He looked at Roberts. 'A sacrificial lamb on the altar of Nathaniel Callaghan. Do you want him to go?'

Roberts nodded.

'Good bye, Mr Maskell,' said Blizzard with a cheerful smile. 'Best wishes to Nathaniel. Good luck explaining this to him. I believe he's a very understanding man when you get to know him. If you're lucky, he'll let you have one of his Belgian biscuits. They're very nice, they are.'

The lawyer bit his lip, stood up and left the room. Once, he had gone, Blizzard turned back to Mark Roberts.

'If you need protection, we can offer it,' said the inspector.

'Like George Killick was protected?' said Roberts sourly. 'DCI Glover told Killick he could protect him but it didn't do him much good, did it? He still got murdered, didn't he?'

'There's a certain irony that you should be the one to remind us of the fact. Besides, I am not Phil Glover. He was in over his head, Mark. I'm not. Give Callaghan up and we can work something out.'

'So, what's the deal?' asked Roberts. 'It had better be good and it had better be now. The moment Maskell gets out of the prison he'll be ringing Callaghan and once Callaghan knows I have been talking to you about him there's no way I'll get out of this place alive. I'll probably not even see the day out.'

'I appreciate that,' said Blizzard. 'Give a statement to us now, saying that Nathaniel Callaghan was involved in the sex ring and the death of George Killick and you can be out of this place within the hour. We can take you to a prison a long way from Hafton and make sure you have a new identity so that no one knows who you are.'

'And my wife and daughter? Callaghan is perfectly capable of hurting them.'

'Full protection.'

'And the murder charge? What will you do about that?'

'I can't let something like that go, Mark,' said Blizzard. I mean, you *did* kill him but maybe we could swing something to get you as short a sentence as possible. Put a word in with the judge. Say you were acting under duress. Who knows, you could be out in ten?'

The inspector looked at Randall, who nodded his agreement. Roberts pursed his lips.

'So, what exactly do I gain?' he asked. 'I mean, I'll still be in prison, won't I?'

'Indeed so, but if you don't help us, we'll charge you anyway,' said Blizzard. 'Like the estimable Mr Maskell so aptly pointed out, you really don't have much manoeuvring room, Mark.'

Roberts sighed heavily.

'OK,' he said. 'I'll talk.'

* * *

An hour later, Blizzard and Randall were standing in the prison car park.

'Got him,' said Randall, patting his friend on the back. 'We've only gone and got Nathaniel Callaghan.'

'If he doesn't get us first.' Blizzard lowered his voice even though no one was near. 'Nathaniel Callaghan is not a man who takes lightly to something like this. If the last two days have taught us anything, Max, it's that no one is safe.'

His mobile phone rang.

'Speak of the devil,' murmured the inspector.

'It's Nathaniel Callaghan,' said a voice. 'You and I need to talk.'

'And what do we need to talk about?' asked Blizzard calmly.

'Don't play fucking games with me,' rasped Callaghan. Gone was the urbane manner of their meeting in Leeds, to be replaced by a tone laden with menace. 'You know exactly what we need to talk about, Blizzard. If you think you're going to get away with this, you're very much mistaken. There's no way that toerag will live to give evidence against me.'

'We'll see about that,' said Blizzard.

'Meet me down by the old warehouse off Marshall Street in two hours,' said Callaghan. 'And don't try anything funny because if you do, so help me…'

He did not finish the threat and the line went dead.

'I have just talked to the real Nathaniel Callaghan,' said Blizzard, unlocking his car door and giving Randall the faintest of smiles. 'And somehow I don't think he'll be offering me any nice biscuits again. Belgian or not.'

The inspector dialled a number.

'Gerry,' he said. 'Blizzard. Listen, do me a favour, will you? Get a couple of uniforms to check my house, make sure Fee and the little 'un are OK.'

Chapter twenty

I did not know what to expect when I met Nathaniel Callaghan again. The man could have had me killed, I knew that, but I was desperate to find out what he had to say. I suspected he would threaten me, but it did strike me that there may be useful information to be had. If I survived. The time had come to put an end to the secrets. To bring Keeper to an end.

'I'm going to meet Nathaniel Callaghan alone, Arthur,' said Blizzard as they sat in the superintendent's office. 'And that's final.'

'No, it's too dangerous.' Ronald looked at his friend with anxiety etched onto his face. 'The chief thinks the same. Thinks you need back-up in case Callaghan does anything stupid.'

'I appreciate his concern.' Blizzard thought for a moment. 'You know, far be it for me to admit that I may have been wrong, but I have started to view the chief in a more positive light over recent days. Perhaps we are on the same side, after all.'

'Always were, John, always were. Whoever it was protecting the sex ring, it wasn't the chief. It was only you who thought that, but you were as wrong can be.'

'How can you be so sure?'

'Because he knew about Keeper right from the off.'

Blizzard stared at him in amazement.

'He did what?' he said.

'It was his idea. Do you really think that boring old Arthur Ronald was going to jeopardise his police pension running something like that without the chief knowing?'

Blizzard looked hurt.

'Why didn't you tell me this earlier?' he said. 'Or any of us? Couldn't you trust us?'

'The chief told me not to. He always suspected that there was someone inside the force protecting the ring, he just didn't know who. He agreed with me that running a covert inquiry was the best way forward.'

'So, all this stuff about him not liking me is all an act?'

'Not quite,' said Ronald with a smile. 'He still thinks you're a bloody liability when the mood gets you. But *I* trust you and that's good enough for him. Same with the others.'

The superintendent looked up at the wall clock.

'Anyway, we can talk about this later,' he said. 'You'll be late for Nathaniel and I don't imagine he's the type of man to tolerate that.'

Blizzard reached for his mug of tea, took a couple of final gulps and stood up.

'I imagine not,' he said. 'I still want to go alone, though. Nothing funny, Nathaniel said.'

'You're a stubborn man,' sighed Ronald. 'Before you go, what's happening with Forrester? You've chosen a high-risk strategy. I had all on to get the chief to agree to it.'

'I know, but if Rachel *has* told Forrester that Alex will take his secrets to the grave, he has got to move against anyone else who may be on his death list.'

'Can't we just arrest Forrester now? Sweat it out of him?'

'On what grounds, Arthur? Visiting someone in prison? Being a mean bastard? We were skating on thin ice when we lifted him last time. The last thing we want is D'Arcy getting him out. No, this is the only way to do it. Besides, even if we lift Forrester, he's highly unlikely to tell us who the gunman is, old pro that he is.'

* * *

Half an hour later, John Blizzard pulled his car onto the weed-strewn wasteland behind Marshall Street. Having guided the vehicle across the rutted truck, its tyres crunching over loose stones, he arrived at the old warehouse, which stood gaunt and skeletal thirty metres from the banks of the Haft, its walls plastered with obscene graffiti, its windows long since smashed by vandals' stones, its interior ripped apart by thieves.

Blizzard cut the engine. He was early. Sitting in silence, he tried to calm his breathing but was conscious that his palms were sweaty and that his pulse seemed to have quickened. He could feel a headache coming on. The inspector got out of the car and walked over to the river's edge, hoping that staring out over the dark waters of the Haft would calm him down, as it had done so often in the past.

Standing there on the riverside path, the city seemed a world away, the sound of the steady stream of vehicles on the nearby bypass a distant hum, and the inspector's mind ranged over the events of his career. Faces flashed before his eyes, criminals he had arrested, victims he had helped, officers with whom he had served. Arthur Ronald's worried frown, David Colley's quirky grin, Max Randall's hangdog demeanour, Alex Mather's inscrutable stare. Blizzard wondered if this was how it was when you prepared for death but, for all his fears, and it was not the first time he had confronted the possibility of dying in the line of duty, this time felt different. This time he felt more vulnerable. Less in control. The inspector thought for a moment and realised why as Rachel Mather's words came back to him. *Have you ever thought about packing it all in? Being a dad is a big responsibility. What would happen to your son if some harm befell you like it did Alex?*

Blizzard shook his head. There was still work to do and he still could not believe that Nathaniel Callaghan would be so reckless as to kill a police officer. For all that belief, John Blizzard felt more alone than he had ever been as the chill wind blew in off the water. He had not been there long when a black saloon with darkened windows crunched its way across the wasteland and pulled up next to the inspector's car. A grim-faced Nathaniel Callaghan got out and was joined by two of his heavies. The inspector walked over to meet him.

'You have been causing me a lot of problems,' said Callaghan in a thin-lipped voice. 'I don't like people who cause me problems, Chief Inspector. It seems that I have underestimated you.'

'You wouldn't be the first to have done that.' Blizzard was relieved that his voice was steady. 'Besides, it was your damn fool mistake that got me thinking in the first place. If you hadn't asked to see me about your junkie grandson, I wouldn't have started thinking that you were covering something else up.'

'Well, I won't be making any more mistakes, I can assure you,' said Callaghan. His voice was quiet. Cold. Menacing. 'Like I said on the phone, Mark Roberts will never testify against me and without him, you have nothing.'

Blizzard glanced at the river.

'Is he going for a swim?' he said. 'Must be getting pretty crowded down there, Nathaniel.'

'Don't make jokes, Chief Inspector!'

'So, is Mark Roberts right?' asked Blizzard. 'Did you put up the cash to have George Killick murdered?'

'You think I'd be that stupid to tell you?' said Callaghan. 'I told you, just because I made one mistake it doesn't mean I'll be making any more. Don't think I don't know what you offered Roberts to testify? I always get to find out. I have my sources.'

'Yes, I've been meaning to ask.' Blizzard was beginning to enjoy himself despite the danger. He sensed that Callaghan was experiencing a mixture of frustration and intrigue that Blizzard was not behaving like the police officers he normally met. 'See, we always thought you had a copper in your pocket. Who is it? My money's on Phil Glover.'

Callaghan did not reply but the slightest flicker of recognition ran across the face.

'Thought so,' sad Blizzard. 'Go on, let me hear it from your own mouth. I'm not wearing a wire. There's no way of confirming what you said, Nathaniel. And it won't stand up in court. I'm entirely alone.'

Callaghan looked round at the deserted wasteland.

'So it would seem,' he said.

'Did you put out the contract on George Killick?'

'What if I did?'

Blizzard looked at him intently.

'You are a man of strange conflicts, Nathaniel,' he said. 'You go to church every Sunday and you hate drugs, yet you think nothing of putting up ten grand to kill George Killick. I never had you down as a paedophile.'

'Not me.' The reply was vehement, the first time Callaghan's veneer had cracked. 'I do not do that kind of thing.'

'Then why put the money up?'

'Sometimes you have to keep people sweet, Chief Inspector. As you yourself observed the last time we met, I have some influential friends but, to keep them friendly, sometimes you need to do them a favour. Keep their names out of certain things.'

'So there were more involved in the sex ring?'

'You don't need to know,' said Callaghan. He turned to look at his heavies who were standing by the car. 'Anyway,

I am warning you off. You are in a dangerous line of work. It's worth remembering that. You saw what happened to your DC Mather.'

'Yes, but I don't think that was your handiwork, Nathaniel. Indeed, as I recall, you were going to give me a name for the shooter.'

'You've got a nerve!' exclaimed Callaghan. 'I said I'd only let you have the name if you dropped the charges against my grandson.'

Blizzard started walking towards his car.

'True enough,' he said over his shoulder. 'And since I assume I am not going for a swim with the fishes, I'll bid you good day.'

Callaghan watched him go, unable to conceal his surprise; he was not used to people walking away from him. They usually waited to be dismissed from his presence.

'Lennie Finch,' he said.

Blizzard gave a slight smile, turned and walked back to Callaghan.

'What did you say?' asked the inspector; the devil within him wanted to make Callaghan utter it again.

'Your gunman is a man called Lennie Finch. Oh, and before you start thinking that you've beaten me at my own game, I'm only telling you because it just so happens that eradicating him would do me a favour.'

'Nothing to do with the fact that my Chief Constable refuses to go easy on drug dealers then?' Blizzard's time to smile. 'Anyway, how does it help you if we lift the gunman?'

'You don't need to know.'

'It's about the guns, I assume?' said Blizzard, trying to sound laconic and enjoying the look of surprise on Callaghan's face.

'How the…?'

'I have my sources,' said Blizzard, with a sly grin. 'We know that someone is trying to set himself up against you.

I imagine you can't have customers thinking you are vulnerable. I don't suppose terrorists do vulnerable.'

'And do you know who it is?'

'Known for a couple of days. Didn't know the name of the gunman, though, although I'm not sure it helps your grandson. I imagine he'll still be charged. Pretty boy like that should do well in prison.'

Callaghan glowered at him.

'What if I told you more?' he said. 'About Finch?'

'I guess that might help. He is not a pro as far as I know. I've certainly never heard of him.'

'I think you will find that none of the pros are stupid enough to get involved with someone who is trying to take me down. I can be a vengeful man, Chief Inspector.'

'Who would have thought it? So, who is Finch? Where did Forrester find him?'

'I understand they have known each for several years. Finch owes Forrester a lot of money from his money-lending business. Forrester threatened his family so Finch has no option but to help. Will you put a word in for my grandson?'

'Can't make any promises, Nathaniel. Maybe. Do you know where we can find Finch?'

'Sorry.' Callaghan turned to go; he was determined that this time it would be his turn to leave. 'You'll get no more from me.'

'And Forrester?' asked Blizzard as Callaghan walked towards his vehicle. 'What will happen to him?'

Callaghan turned round.

'The man has no class,' he said with a faint smile. 'You have to have class in this business.'

'So, what *will* happen to him?'

Callaghan glanced at his heavies, one of whom had opened the car door for him.

'It's all a question of who catches up with him first,' he said. 'You or my boys. For his sake, he'd better hope it's you. I'm not bothered either way, though. As long as he's out of the way I'm happy. Until next time, Chief Inspector.'

'And there will be a next time,' said Blizzard.

Callaghan turned and gave Blizzard a slight smile.

'Take nothing for granted, Chief Inspector,' he said. 'You be careful now.'

Blizzard watched as the car headed off across the wasteland. Experiencing a rising feeling of unease as the comment triggered his instinct for danger, he turned to get into his own vehicle. As he did so, another car approached across the wasteland. The inspector felt a knot of fear in his stomach as the vehicle pulled up and a young man got out, holding a handgun.

'Lennie Finch, I assume,' said Blizzard, trying to sound calm.

'So, you know who I am,' said Finch, raising the gun. 'Much good may it do you.'

Three police officers carrying firearms emerged from the nearby copse.

'Armed police!' shouted one. 'Drop your weapon!'

Finch whirled round to stare in horror at the guns trained on him.

'Do as I say!' shouted the officer. 'I'll not warn you again!'

Finch turned back to Blizzard, hesitated then pulled the trigger and the gun kicked in his hand. The bullet slammed into Blizzard's chest and the inspector gave a grunt of pain and slumped to his knees before pitching over to lie still. A shot rang out and Finch lurched to one side then collapsed. His body twitched for a moment then was still.

There was a squeal of tyres and two cars appeared from the direction of the warehouse and sped over to where Blizzard was lying motionless. Moving quicker than anyone could remember seeing, Ronald jumped out of the first vehicle and ran over to his friend. As he stared down at Blizzard, the inspector groaned, sat up and rubbed his chest, wincing at the discomfort.

'It was me then,' said Blizzard ruefully, accepting the superintendent's helping hand as he hauled himself to his feet. He watched as the armed officers crouched over Finch's body. 'I was the other name on the list.'

'So, it would seem.' Ronald looked at him with relief written across his face. 'I told you that you needed back-up.'

Blizzard gave a lopsided grin.

'And you're never wrong, eh?' he said.

'No, and don't you forget it. You appear to be in pretty good shape for a dead man. It suits you.' The superintendent reached over and tapped the bullet-proof vest that the inspector was wearing beneath his coat. 'Good job we decided that CID should wear these until all this was sorted, although your hide is that thick, the bullet would probably have bounced off anyway.'

Blizzard rubbed his chest again.

'Yes, thanks for that,' he said. 'What happened to respect for the dead?'

Colley got out of the second car.

'Forrester?' shouted the inspector.

'Surveillance followed him to a pub on Clay Street. They're waiting for us there.'

* * *

Twenty minutes later, Ronnie Forrester had just left the back-street city centre pub when several armed police officers appeared from nearby shop doorways and trained their weapons on him.

'On your knees!' shouted a man's voice.

Stunned by the speed of the operation, Forrester did as he was told and moments later, he squealed with pain as his arms were twisted behind his back. As he was hauled to his feet and taken towards a police van that had driven into the street, a familiar figure appeared and walked over to him.

'You're supposed to be dead,' gasped Forrester.

'Apparently,' said Blizzard as the armed officers brought Forrester to a halt. He rubbed his chest. 'Being dead doesn't half smart, I can tell you.'

'Well, I ain't saying nowt!'

'You don't need to, Ronnie. Finch is dead and we're off to nick your murderous girlfriend. Oh, and I've just had a nice little chat with Nathaniel Callaghan about you. Enjoy prison, Ronnie.'

Forrester did not reply but the fear in his eyes did the speaking for him. Blizzard gave a satisfied smile and the image of a young girl with a needle in her arm came into his mind. Payback.

As Forrester was taken away by the armed officers, he glanced back towards the pub and saw Eddie Gayle watching him impassively through the window.

Chapter twenty-one

Sister Maitland walked over to Rachel Mather as she entered the intensive care unit.

'Is he still alive?' asked Rachel, a worried look on her face as he glanced over towards her brother's bed.

'Sorry to scare you, lovey,' said the nurse. 'He's stabilised again. God willing, he's turned the corner.'

Rachel walked over to the unconscious figure of her brother.

'You mean he might live?' she said.

'The doctors think he may, yes.' Sister Maitland smiled brightly. 'He's not out of the woods yet but we can be cautiously optimistic. That's good news, isn't it?'

'It's such a relief,' said Rachel but her voice sounded flat.

'I'll leave you to have some quiet time with your brother,' said the Sister and walked out into the corridor. She had not been gone but a few seconds when a grim-faced Arthur Ronald entered the room.

'Alex may be over the worst of…' began Rachel but her voice tailed off on seeing his solemn expression. 'What's wrong, Arthur?'

Ronald sat down heavily next to the bed.

'John Blizzard was on the gunman's list as well,' he said quietly. 'He was shot dead half an hour ago.'

Rachel clapped a hand to her mouth.

'God, no,' she said. 'His poor girlfriend. And the baby.'

'Such a tragedy,' said Ronald, trying to avoid his revulsion at her play-acting. 'I'm heading off there now, but I thought that you'd want to know.'

They sat in silence for a few moments.

'Did you get the man who did it?' asked Rachel eventually.

'I am afraid not, but we are pretty sure it was the same man that shot your brother.' Ronald stood up and looked across at Mather. 'God knows why he did it. If Alex is over the worst, hopefully he can give us some of the answers when he comes round. He's the only one who can.'

'I do hope so,' said Rachel as the superintendent reached the door. 'I'm very sorry about John. He was a fine man and he did not deserve to die like this.'

'It comes with the territory, I am afraid,' said Ronald. He nodded at Mather. 'Just ask your brother, he knows that only too well. I am glad he is starting to recover, Rachel, I really am.'

When he had gone, Rachel sat in silence for a few moments then glanced around the intensive care unit. Noticing that there was only one nurse there and that she was busy with another patient at the far end of the room, Rachel stood up and walked over to Mather. She hesitated for another moment, took another glance in the direction of the nurse and picked up a pillow lying on a nearby chair. She leaned over the bed.

'Sorry, brother, dear,' she murmured. Tears ran down her cheeks. 'But needs must when the devil drives.'

'I wouldn't do that,' said a voice and she whirled round to see Blizzard walking across the room. The inspector held out a hand. 'Give me the pillow.'

'But you're dead!' she exclaimed.

'People keep telling me that. If this carries on, I'll get a complex about it.' The inspector reached over and took the pillow from her. 'It's over, Rachel, we've got Finch and Forrester and now we've got you.'

'Ronnie made me do it,' she said, bursting into tears. 'You have to believe me, Ronnie forced me to do it.'

'Tell it to the judge,' said Blizzard.

Chapter twenty-two

'And she admitted all this, did she?' asked Alex Mather, unable to conceal the note of disbelief in his voice. 'My sister admitted that she was prepared to see me killed?'

It was four days after Rachel Mather's arrest and the detective was sitting up in his bed, in a side room at the hospital. Blizzard, who was sitting on a chair next to the bed, nodded sadly.

'I am afraid so,' he said. 'I am truly sorry, Alex, I really wish I could say otherwise.'

Mather digested the information for a few moments then shook his head, wincing slightly at the stab of pain that the movement caused.

'I just can't believe it,' he said. He lay back on his pillow and closed his eyes. 'I really can't.'

Blizzard surveyed his friend's pale complexion and stood up.

'I'll come back later,' he said. 'I'm not sure you're up to this yet.'

Mather opened his eyes.

'No, please stay,' he said.

Blizzard sat back down again.

'You know,' said Mather after a few more moments' silence, 'I have spent my career priding myself on my ability to spot those people you can trust. It's how I kept myself alive for ten years undercover but I never suspected my own sister. Not in a million years.'

'I wouldn't beat yourself up about it, Alex, she had us all fooled.'

'I guess I'm not surprised she took up with someone like Forrester, mind. She's always had a thing for a bit of rough, has Rachel. She had some dodgy boyfriends before she got married and her husband was no angel. All tattoos and dead brain cells. How did she meet Forrester?'

'They got talking in a club and my guess is that when Forrester discovered the link with you, he saw a golden opportunity. She's really very naive is your sister.'

'She always was,' said Mather. 'I have always been warning her off doing daft things. She damn near signed for a timeshare in Spain that didn't exist until I heard about it. But this? Never saw this coming, John. I guess it was because of poor Aidan?'

'We think so. When Forrester found out that Aidan was going to tell you about the guns, it was easy enough for him to get your address off Rachel.'

'And she knew then that he planned to have me killed?'

Blizzard hesitated.

'Tell me the truth, John,' said Mather. 'Please.'

'We think she did, yes,' said Blizzard with a sigh. 'She told us that she didn't dare try to stop him but I still reckon she thought he'd pay off her debts if he made a lot of money from the guns.'

'No wonder she was evasive when I asked her if she had a new boyfriend.' Mather closed his eyes and lay silent for a few moments then opened them and looked at Blizzard. 'Sorry you got roped into this.'

'It's the job, you know that. *Had* Aidan told you?'

'No, but he had asked to see me the day after I was shot. We were due to meet in the afternoon.'

'All a waste of time, really. Forrester thought Nathaniel Callaghan knew nothing about his little scheme but he had already planned to take care of business. Now, he can sit back and let us do his dirty work for him.'

'But surely you've got Callaghan in the frame for ordering the murder of George Killick?' asked Mather.

'There's a reason Nathaniel Callaghan never sees the inside of a courtroom, Alex. I'm just letting the lawyers get on with it. Bad for my blood pressure if I get involved.'

Mather was silent, then a thought struck him.

'Why did Rachel not finish me off when she found me at the cottage?' he said, looking hopeful. 'Perhaps she had second thoughts?'

'Wish I could say you're right, but she thought you'd be dead. When you weren't, she decided it would look better if she let you live and raised the alarm. Deflect attention away from her. She told us she thought you would die before regaining consciousness anyway so her secret would still be safe.'

'It's like I never ever really knew her.'

'Oddly enough, she said the same thing about you.'

Silence settled on the room again as Mather struggled to process what he had been told.

'What about Eddie Gayle?' he asked eventually. 'Have you charged him with setting up the murder of George Killick?'

'How can we? All we can prove is that he visited a bad lad in prison. For a while we had him in the frame for hiring the gunman who shot you, though. We suspected he may have rung you just before the attack to check you were in.'

'Why think that?' Mather sounded more guarded now.

'Because we found your mobile phone number on a scrap of paper in a drawer at his home.'

'Ah.'

Blizzard looked hard at his friend. Something in the way Mather had spoken hinted at truths unspoken.

'How come Eddie Gayle has got your number, Alex?' he asked.

'Because for the past ten tears, Eddie Gayle has been my best informant.'

Blizzard stared at him in astonishment.

'You are kidding?' he said. 'Eddie Gayle passing on information? But he hates the police!'

'He does indeed but your arch enemy has actually been responsible for putting away some of the biggest villains in this city.'

'In return for what? His name does not appear on your list of paid informants.'

'I didn't pay him in money.'

Blizzard looked hard at him.

'What did you pay him in?' he said. 'Something you want to tell me?'

'Like what?' Mather's tone was even more guarded now.

'Like we always suspected that someone inside the force has been leaking information. First, I thought it was the chief, then we thought it might be Phil Glover and…'

'And now you think it might be me tipping Gayle off.' Mather looked at his friend intently. 'Is that it, John? Me betraying my friends? All those years undercover made me forget whose side I'm on?'

'I have to ask.'

'You know me better than that. No, Eddie's motives are far less complicated. With his rivals out of the picture, who is there to stop him?'

Blizzard shook his head.

'You can shake your head all you like,' said Mather. He closed his eyes. 'But sometimes the ends justify the means. Think of everyone I nicked thanks to Eddie. Leaving him at large was a price I was prepared to pay.'

'Did Andy Barratt know?'

'Nobody did. Look, I can see why a lot of people would disapprove of what I did but the city is better for it.

There's even a phrase for it: noble cause corruption. I went to a course on it once.'

'Well, it doesn't wash in my world, Alex.' Blizzard thought of all the victims of Eddie Gayle that he had dealt with down the years, thought of a badly beaten young girl lying in a seedy bedsit with a needle dangling from her arm. He stood up. 'Sorry, it doesn't wash at all and, as for your pal, it stops and it stops now.'

But Alex Mather was asleep.

* * *

Once Blizzard was back in the car park, he checked the contacts list on his mobile phone and stood deep in thought for a few moments as families streamed past him on their way into the hospital for visiting hours. The inspector remembered the sound of Finch's gun and the screams of terrified people fleeing across the car park for their lives. Remembered again, as he had done so many times since he had first heard it, the primeval shriek of Aidan Horan's girlfriend staring down in horror as the blood gushed from his body. Without knowing he had done it, Blizzard gave a nod of the head and dialled a number.

'Eddie Gayle,' said a voice.

'Blizzard,' said the inspector.

'What the hell do you want?'

'I've just been talking to Alex Mather and guess what he told me?'

There was silence at the other end.

'I just wanted you to know that your deal with him is over,' continued Blizzard.

'I don't know what you are talking about,' said Gayle.

'Oh, I'm sure you do, Eddie,' said Blizzard. 'And I wanted you to know that from now on, you are fair game. See, in my world, no one is untouchable.'

Chapter twenty-three

'So that's the story of my death,' said Blizzard, finishing his account and taking a sip of tea from the bone china cup as he waited for the Chief Constable's reaction. 'In all its glory.'

'And very interesting it was, too,' said the chief. 'Arthur Ronald does not tell me the half of it, you know. No wonder the man is getting an ulcer. Tell me, what do *you* think I should do with Alex Mather?'

'I can't agree that he was right to help Eddie Gayle build his empire and I've already put a stop to it, but as for what we do with him…' The inspector's voiced tailed off. Rarely did he find himself stuck for words but he had found himself wrestling more and more with the ramifications of Mather's actions and now the chief inspector did not know how to finish the sentence.

'It is certainly a tricky one,' said the chief. He glanced at a piece of paper lying on his desk. 'Out of interest, I asked Andy Barratt how many crooks have been put away thanks in part to information from Alex. Thirteen pimps, nine major drug dealers, six men for people trafficking, two for murder, one for attempted murder… I could go on.'

'But he got too close, sir,' said Blizzard, his affection for Mather outweighed by revulsion for Eddie Gayle. 'Went out on his own. Wouldn't be the first time that's happened to a copper.'

'No, indeed. It seems that his handlers were too fixated on results when he was undercover to see what they were doing to the man.'

'Can you blame them? You do have a thing about results, sir.'

'You like it when they're going in your favour, I think,' said the chief with a sly smile. 'However, don't blame me, blame the Home Office and their fresh-faced pen-pushers just out of kindergarten. Perhaps, I'm getting too old for this lark. I could take early retirement next year. It's tempting. I do not want to spend the next five years jumping every time they say jump. Talking of kindergarten, how's that boy of yours?'

'Fine, sir, thank you.'

'Good. So, what *would* you, the new more human John Blizzard, do with Alex Mather?'

'I am not sure I'd discipline him.'

'No, nor me,' said the chief. He gave Blizzard another sly smile, surprising the chief inspector, who had always regarded him as a humourless man. 'Otherwise, we'd all be in trouble. You for running what you thought was an operation away from your chief constable's prying eyes and me for rampant corruption in public office.'

Blizzard gave him a rueful look.

'I've already apologised for that, sir,' he said.

'So you have. So you have. You don't think Alex was leaking information to Eddie Gayle then? Or to the members of the sex ring for that matter?'

Blizzard shook his head.

'Was Phil Glover?' asked the chief, a glint of mischief in his eyes.

'You heard then?'

'I hear everything, Chief Inspector. Worth remembering that. So, *do* you think DCI Glover is crooked?'

'On balance, I probably think that Phil is on the level.'

'Yes, you're probably right. Not enough imagination, that one.' The chief took a sip of tea. 'OK, I'll go to the hospital and have a quiet word with Alex Mather. Nothing formal. From what I hear he may be trying to get back with his wife and may stay on with the force for a few months to see how it goes.'

'That's true, yes, sir.'

'Good. His methods may be unorthodox – and the kiddywinks in the Home Office would not approve, that's for sure – but he does catch criminals. As do you.' The chief constable sat back in his chair and surveyed the detective for a few moments, another look of faint amusement on his face. 'What on earth do I do with you?'

'I'd let me keep doing what I do.'

'I'm sure you would but you're a loose cannon. I spend more time handling complaints about you than any senior officer.' The chief noticed Blizzard's worried expression and wafted a hand in his direction. 'OK, on your way. Just check with me first the next time you decide to call me corrupt, yes?'

Blizzard stood up.

'You have my word,' he said solemnly.

He had reached the door when the chief spoke again.

'That sergeant of yours?' he said. 'David Colley?'

Blizzard turned back into the room.

'What about him?' he asked.

'Arthur tells me he has declined the opportunity of promotion to uniformed inspector. Arthur reckons that he would rather stay as detective sergeant in Western CID?'

'Yes, that's right, sir.'

'Any idea why?'

'I think it's something about my sparkling personality,' said Blizzard.

The chief clicked his fingers in recognition.

'Ah, of course,' he said. 'That'll be it. Good day, Chief Inspector.'

'Good day, sir. And thank you.'

Sighing with relief, Blizzard walked out of the office and five minutes later was out in the fresh air. A familiar figure awaited him by his car, holding onto a pushchair.

'You survived then?' said Colley.

'Yeah. Just. What are you doing here? I thought you were on a day off.' Blizzard leaned over the pushchair and grinned at the toddler. 'Hello, Looby.'

The child beamed. Colley looked up at the blue sky.

'I wondered if you fancied a trip to feed the ducks?' he said. 'Down at Rosham Park.'

'I'd love to, David, but I'd better get back. I've got an awful lot of paperw…'

'It's just that Fee is on her way down with Mikey if you do.'

'I seem to have no options left,' said Blizzard with a smile. 'So, yes, I'd love to.'

'That's my boy,' replied Colley.

THE END

List of characters

Hafton Officers:

DCI John Blizzard – head of Western Division CID
DCI Phil Glover – head of Eastern Division CID
DI Max Randall
DI Graham Ross – head of forensics in Western Division
DS David Colley
Sgt Mel Powell
DC Fee Ellis
DC Alex Mather
DC Sarah Allatt
DC Jane Riley

County force:

Det Supt Arthur Ronald – head of CID in the southern half of the force
DI Andy Barratt – head of Force Intelligence Department
Alison Curry – press officer

Others:

Leonard Baines – a travel agent

Nathaniel Callaghan – a villain
Luke Callaghan – his grandson
Paul D'Arcy – a lawyer
Lennie Finch – a villain
Ronnie Forrester – a villain
Eddie Gayle – a villain
Assistant Prison Governor Halford – works at Hafton Prison
Aidan Horan – a drug dealer
George Killick – a convicted paedophile
Barrie Killick – son of George
Bob Maynard – delivery firm owner
Leonard Maskell – a lawyer
Polly Mather – Alex Mather's wife
Rachel Mather – Alex Mather's sister
Peter Reynolds – Home Office Pathologist
Mark Roberts – a prisoner

If you enjoyed this book, please let others know by leaving a quick review on Amazon. Also, if you spot anything untoward in the paperback, get in touch. We strive for the best quality and appreciate reader feedback.

editor@thebookfolks.com

www.thebookfolks.com

ALSO BY JOHN DEAN

In this series:

The Long Dead (Book 1)
Strange Little Girl (Book 2)
The Railway Man (Book 3)
The Secrets Man (Book 4)
A Breach of Trust (Book 5)
A Flicker in the Night (Book 7)
The Latch Man (Book 8)
No Age to Die (Book 9)
The Vengeance Man (Book 10)
The Name on the Bullet (Book 11)

In the DCI Jack Harris series:

Dead Hill
The Vixen's Scream
To Die Alone
To Honour the Dead
Thou Shalt Kill
Error of Judgement
The Killing Line
Kill Shot
Last Man Alive
The Girl in the Meadow

Writing as John Stanley:

The Numbers Game
Sentinel

When a routine archaeological dig turns up bodies on the site of a WWII prisoner of war camp, it should be an open and shut case for detective John Blizzard. But forensics discover one of the deaths is more recent and the force have a murder investigation on their hands.

When a family is brutally murdered, one child is never found. It still troubles DCI John Blizzard to this day. But new clues emerge that will take him deep into the criminal underworld and into conflict with the powers that be. Cracking the case will take all of the detective's skills, and more. Coming out unscarred will be impossible.

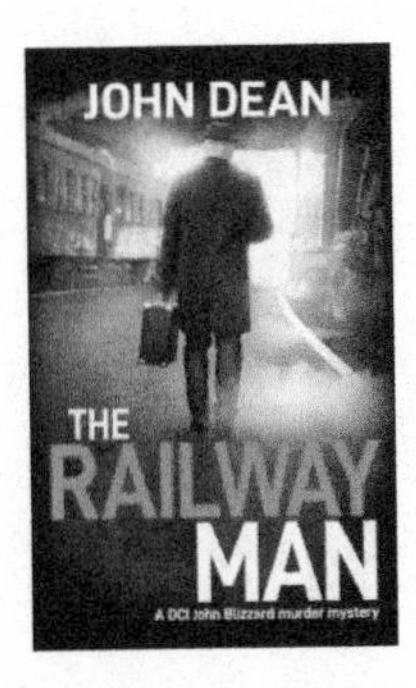

Veteran crime-solver DCI John Blizzard is confronted with his hardest case yet when a boxer and wide boy is found dead in a railway signal box. Someone is determined to ruin the investigation and prepared to draw the residents of a local housing estate into a war with the police to get their way. Has the detective finally met his match?

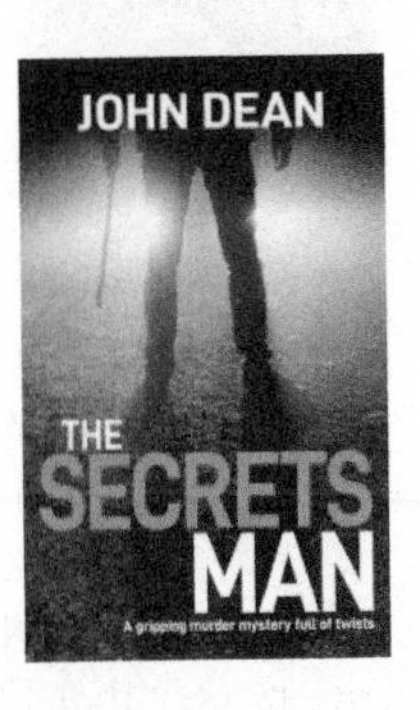

While detective John Blizzard looks into a series of drug-related deaths, his nemesis, gangland thug Morrie Raynor, is released from prison. Blizzard becomes convinced Raynor is linked to a new crime spree, but with little evidence other than the ravings of a sick, delirious man, the detective's colleagues suspect his personal feelings are clouding his judgement.

A corrupt industrialist is found dead in his home. When his family shed crocodile tears, DCI John Blizzard turns the screw. But when their alibis check out, can his team track down the real killer among a long list of likely suspects?

Someone is starting deadly fires, but the only clue to their identity is the obscure poetry that DCI John Blizzard receives on his desk. Taunting the police is one thing. Taunting Blizzard another. He'll stop at nothing to crack the case and collar the arsonist.

No-nonsense detective John Blizzard faces a difficult case when the matriarch of a criminal family is found dead. He must act quick to stop the situation from escalating into a gangland war.

When a dangerous convicted felon is released from prison, DCI Blizzard makes it clear he is unwelcome on his patch. But when a local church takes the man in, Blizzard has to deal with the community uproar. When a local youth is killed it will take all of the detective's skills to right a wrong.

When a youth is scared out of his wits by a man dressed all in black in the local church graveyard, the police don't think much of his tales about a bogeyman. But when a murder later takes place there, DCI John Blizzard will have to suspend disbelief and work out the identity of The Vengeance Man before he wreaks havoc in the neighbourhood.

When a cop taking part in a reality TV show is shot dead, it makes the police look pretty bad. DCI John Blizzard, no media darling himself, sets to finding the killer. This leads him to lock horns with a renowned gangster who acts like he is above the law. Yet as Blizzard tries to balance the scales of justice, he is thrown a curve ball.

Visit www.thebookfolks.com for more great titles like these!

Made in the USA
Middletown, DE
27 February 2024